thri

Exp' your

fears !

:)

TOWN

STEPHEN KOZAN

Illustrated by Tony Maulfair

READYAIMWRITE
PUBLISHING

READYAIMWRITE
PUBLISHING

TOWN
www.TownTheBook.com

Stephen Kozan
Illustrated by Tony Maulfair

www.BookVisits.com
www.StephenKozan.com

First U.S. Edition, 2017

ISBN 978-0-9984661-0-1
LCCN 2017939520

Printed in the U.S.A.

For Cameron and Aubrey

"Friends can be the best co-conspirators in charting the unknown."

— Judith Orloff

CONTENTS

i

TOWN

ONE

FORT BLISS

Whoosh, zip, whoosh, whoosh, zip! "We're taking heavy fire," a panicked voice cries out. "Keep going—don't stop!" Whoosh, whoosh, zip! "I can't see in front of me! Ouch! Rock!" Bullets rip through the dense leaves of the maple trees where the terrorized voices are engulfed. "Nia! Catch up!"

"Kyle, go! I'm—" Zip, whoosh, zip!

"Hey, hey, hey—no way, no stopping!

"I'm hit!" Michael collapses to the ground. The others converge on him. There is raw agony on his face as they kneel beside him. His deep brown eyes gloss over. "I can't feel my legs. I'm not gonna make it, am I? You're the best friends a guy could have."

"Mike, it's a rubber bullet. You're not even bleeding, dude," Skyler says.

Kyle and Nia look at Skyler and roll their eyes.

Lying back, relaxing on the ground, his long black hair fans out, picking up leaves like Velcro. "I thought it was the end," whispers Mike.

Shaking their heads, Kyle, Nia, and Skyler form an arm-bridge around Michael's arms and neck, helping him to his feet. The cacophonic barrage of the rubber bullet siege has stopped, allowing the four friends to carry on at a much more relaxed pace toward their destination.

"Old Man Horner, ay guys? Kyle laughs.

"Old Man Horner," confirms Nia.

One by one, and with great caution, they rappel twenty feet down to their "safe zone," using an old garden hose tied around a thick maple tree.

Cold Creek Forest has become not only a meeting point between the friends, but it is also home to the curmudgeonly stubborn, kid-hating, rubber-bullet-shooting, Old Man Horner. He is a dug-in thorn in the proverbial side of anyone who passes through *his* woods. And his weapon of choice: a rubber bullet gun that shoots marble-sized pellets at the rate of 200 feet per second. It packs some pop, and for certain is a deterrent each time they step foot into the woods.

"Man, your face!" Skyler says. She laughs then throws an arm-length twig at Michael. "You really thought you were dying. Biggest person in our group, and you're about ready to tap out. You goof."

"But it felt li—"

"You know, Old Man Horner shoots at people in his woods," says Kyle, uncomfortably tilting his neck to the side as his hearing aid begins emitting a low-resonance squeak that will soon become a piercing, high-pitched howl.

"Well, I never got hit," Mike replies.

"You did now!" Skyler laughs, clutching at her heart and stumbling as if she has really been shot. Her long, thick, textured, black braid swings over her shoulder. She balls up both dark-skinned fists, bringing them to her eyes, twisting while making an exaggerated crying gesture.

"You guys stink," Mike says.

Staggered, walking in a non-uniform, two-by-two formation, the four friends cross over the makeshift bridge they had built from scrap pieces of plywood and hunks of round stone gathered from the nearby quarry. They needed something to traverse the creek—the last obstacle before reaching their terminus. Though the creek is low-lying, it's a dangerous body of water due to the soft sand and slick silt that lines the bottom. Quicksand is just not to be messed with.

"Up ahead, boys!" shouts Kyle, pointing toward what they came for.

FORT BLISS

It is a structure built *for* kids, *by* kids: *these* kids. The "fort" measures about 12'x12', with sides constructed from secondhand MDO plywood panels they had scavenged from the rear parking lot of a defunct sign company. Attached to the exterior walls of the fort are broken off sections of evergreen branches nailed and glued to the side panels. It forms a densely-constructed tapestry of camouflage, allowing it to blend in with the surrounding foliage. The roof, pieced together and nailed tightly with planks of 2'x4' posts is covered by a dark green tarp tied by nylon rope to trunks of nearby trees. One cool feature of the tarp roof is an improvised skylight that Michael had installed using glass from a discarded moon-

roof he'd found near a dumpsite at the old steel mill. A rickety door, slightly off hinge, has the words FORT BLISS painted in off-white latex; it practically glows against the pale brown color of the MDO boards.

The fort is nestled deep within a patch of tall, gnarled, grumpy-looking maple trees that are flanked by short, straight, happier-looking evergreens. Dotted in between both sets of trees are various unapologetic weeds, shrubs, and crooked tufts of plants that resemble sawgrass. From the air, there is no way you could spot this place due to the forest's impenetrable canopy. On the ground, it is a flawlessly disguised micro-fortress hidden among the giants of the jungle. The perfect location for a fort.

Kyle, Michael, Nia, and Skyler stand with their hands on their hips admiring the beloved fort they had all worked so hard to build. It is home base—their safe zone—a special place for the meeting of the minds, where fear and anxiety take a backseat to bravery and resolution.

Kyle reaches out, grabs the rusty doorknob, turns it three-quarters, looks back at his fellow comrades and makes the traditional FORT BLISS announcement, "Entrée."

One by one, the group files in, each taking a seat on a bulky, fat-bottomed tree stump with their corresponding first initial carved into the face. The only source of light illuminating the musty fort is Michael's skylight, which provides just enough light for everyone to see each other's face.

Kyle brushes aside his overgrown, dirty blonde hair—purposely styled to mask his hearing aid—and adjusts the volume slider on the device, lowering the setting since the fort provides ample acoustics for him to hear the conversation. With a confident posture, and a clearing of his scratchy throat, Kyle straightens—as best he can—his already wrinkled tee shirt.

"Any old business?" Kyle asks. "Any new business?"

Nia is stone-faced and cautious. Her sharp, narrow eyes are accentuated by her high, tight, shiny-black ponytail. With hesitation, she glares at each of her friends before speaking. "So, what do you guys know about the *shadowmen?*"

TWO

THE FLYING TIGERS

Most twelve-year-old kids in 2009 like discussing all the new songs on the radio, the latest gaming consoles and the cool accessories that are included. Others talk about movies, a shoe craze, or which boy likes which girl and vice versa. This group is a little different, though. This group is spellbound by history, particularly World War II.

They are self-proclaimed experts on the subject—thanks to the brave actions of their long-deceased grandfathers. They trade mutually heroic stories about their grand pappies; stories that are often donated by their parents and other family members who knew the old-time war vets. Rare photos found in dusty albums inspire intriguing Saturday afternoon conversations. These gatherings also provide ample time for consumption of sodas and bags of half-eaten corn chips. Both of which Michael wishes they had right now to fill the silence that has followed Nia's question about the shadowmen.

No one knows how to respond. The awkward silence is underscored by the dying day as the sunlight dims through Michael's skylight.

Kyle finally breaks the silence, "You know what I was just reading the other day? It was about World War II and this secret army, well, not an army, but this, like, squadron of United States volunteers who flew planes. Well, okay, officially they *weren't* Americans, they were Chinese. Well they *were* Americans but fighting *for* the Chinese against the Japanese."

Skyler shakes her head and shoots a glance at Nia, putting her index finger to the side of her ear and twirling it in a circular motion while rolling her big brown eyes.

Kyle glares at Skyler. "I can see you!" He throws his hands up. "Look, okay, so this American-Chinese squadron who fought against the Japanese, they called themselves something. Nia, you're Chinese, you should know this."

"Kyle just because I'm Chi—"

"*The Flying Tigers*," says Skyler.

"Yeah, girl! Exactly," shouts Kyle.

"My grandfather Claude knew of them—at least that's what I was told," Skyler says. "He was a red-tail. My dad used to talk about my grandfather a lot. He was a big deal back then with the Tuskegee Airmen."

"Tuskegee Airman!?" blurts Michael.

"Yeah, a real big deal. My grandfather told my dad about The Flying Tigers, and how they

12

were the first American volunteer group of the Chinese Air Force…even though they were Americans. It's weird, I know. But anyway, they had this cool logo on their planes like shark teeth, the mouth of a shark on the nose of their planes. They flew these secret operations and stuff. It sounded wild."

"That could be us!" shouts Nia.

"She's right," says Skyler. "I like it. We're a group, like a squadron. We don't fly, but we're volunteers for our town. We're trying to find out what the heck is going on. *We* hold secret operations."

"Listen," Kyle says. "I don't want to pop your parade balloons, but we meet in a recycled fort outfitted with pine branches and a door that's clinging to life-support."

"Don't forget my skylight," quips Michael.

"Stop it. Let's be real here," says Skyler. "We *are* like them. We *know* strange things are happening in our town. We're the only ones who seem to care enough to try to find out what exactly is going on. Ever since the nuclear accident on Marathon Island thirty years ago, and then the steel mill closing, things haven't been the same. And, Nia, I didn't want to admit this earlier because I wanted *you* to be the crazy one, but *I have seen the shadowmen too.*"

Nia's head might as well have just detonated. "I knew it!"

The dying light above Michael's moonroof is signaling another end to a successful meeting at Fort Bliss. All four look up, noticing that the fading sunbeams are changing from lavender to blue, which means it's time to high-tail it through Old Man Horner's war-torn woodlands.

"We gotta go," says Kyle.

The four friends rise in unison from their fat-bottomed tree stumps, and walk toward the door. Kyle is the last to exit. He turns the rusted doorknob three-quarters counterclockwise and inserts the long bolt to lock it up.

"You think Horner's trigger finger is still

twitching?" asks Michael.

"That fool is asleep by now. There's no way he stays awake past nine o'clock. He's too old and cranky!" replies Skyler.

"I agree," Kyle says.

"Me three," says Nia.

In the same, staggered, two-by-two formation in which they had entered Old Man Horner's woods, the group negotiates their way back. All the while batting maple tree branches away from their faces.

While crossing the creek bridge, Kyle gets curious. "Hey, Skyler—whatever happened to The Flying Tigers anyhow?"

"Disbanded. 1942. Taken over by another Air Force fighter group. That's what pop told me."

Kyle nods.

"But, hey—you know what?" she continues. "That shark logo they had, they ended up using it for other fighter plane groups because the Flying Tigers had made such an

15

impact."

As if having finally stumbled upon a pallet of unicorn dust—something she frequently rants about wishing would happen—firecracker Nia shouts from the rear, "*We* can make an impact!"

Everyone spins around.

"*Shhhhhhhhh!*" Michael hisses. "The only thing making an impact right now is going to be Old Man Horner's rubber bullets if you don't keep quiet!"

Nia pumps her fist. "Yeah, *impact*," she whispers to herself.

Nia keeps quiet until they are almost through the maze of maples, a few short steps away from emerging onto the cracked pavement of Center Street. It's just in time too, because the sun has officially dipped below the horizon, and the faint remaining light is gracefully saying its final goodnight.

Before splitting into different directions toward their homes, the four friends dust off their shirts and pants, scraping any remaining mud caked onto the bottoms of their shoes off on the curb.

"Whaddya think, ya'll?" says Michael. "The Flying Tigers?"

Skyler looks at Kyle. "The Flying Tigers."

Kyle nods. "The Flying Tigers."

They all glance toward Nia, whose head resembles an over-stuffed piñata. Arms raised, she finally has her moment, *"THE FLYING TIGERS!"*

THREE

WHITE TANKS

For most towns in Pennsylvania, typical summertime Sunday mornings are reserved for the chirping of birds, the kiss of sunlight through double-paned windows, and slow breezes carrying a bouquet of thriving garden scents. Strangers wave to other strangers in parks. Car horns toot at passing joggers distracted by their wireless headphones. Dogs chase chipped Frisbees thrown by overzealous parents. Neighbors dressed in cotton robes sit atop their decks in gravity chairs, reading the newspaper, sipping piping-hot coffee from a mug labeled #1 Dad. First graders eager to play under the powder-blue sky fumble through backyard sheds to retrieve scooters for street racing. But this isn't a typical town.

This is White Tanks. A town still recovering from the nearby nuclear meltdown on Marathon Island, and for some pockets of town, thirty years ago might as well have been just yesterday.

White Tanks is miles from any bustling city, secluded in its own secrecy and demise. It is a place that even morbid tourists have grown tired of scrutinizing. Dying sycamore trees line unkempt roads connected to alleys that look as if they were carpet-bombed by B-52's. Houses with crooked shutters, corroded sewer grates, and rusted fire hydrants with chipped paint frame the scene.

A deserted playground void of smiling laughing children has become a necropolis of bulky metal sculptures coated in faded, worn paint, scored with the coded gang slangs of childhood wonderment lost too soon. A seahorse with a worn-away saddle and broken coil—no longer able to sway—keeps watch over the basketball hoop rims with tattered or missing nets. Some crooked poles support backboards bowed at the edges, as if hugging the wind and rain that had betrayed them. Curb weeds exploit cracks in the asphalt that have given way to wild, late night gatherings where each sprout dances wildly, ignoring curfew because no one cares enough to evict them.

Not many residents are seen outside, choosing to evade whatever hazy sun filters through the cloud cover. Lawns in mottled shades of green and brown offer patches of thick grass in varying lengths and blade thickness, as if mimicking an elderly man's beard that's well past the point of vanity.

Large chunks of stone are missing from the local auto body shop's concrete walls, and the awning bearing its name is faded to the point where one can hardly make out the words "Randy's Garage." What remains of the once beloved Bob's Candy Confections is now closed, and has become target practice for outsiders trained in paintball graffiti who think it's cool to shoot the place up under the cover of twilight. Its once glittery masonry block now has blackened streaks of acid rain damage. Beyond the splatters of exploded paintball bullets are jagged smashed windows—glass shards scattered below, like misfit jigsaw puzzle pieces that no one saw fit to put back together.

Down the main road, about a mile from Kyle's house, is the permanently closed Duggan Brothers Steel Mill. In its heyday, the mill was responsible for seventy-five percent of White Tanks' work force. Dads and granddads with navy colored, starched-collar Dickies shirts— sleeves rolled up to their elbows, would kiss their family's goodbye, grab their lunch pail, and head off for a grueling shift overseeing 2500-degree cauldrons of molten steel, only to return 10-hours later with sweaty armpits, helmet-visor indentions in their forehead, and a stomach ready to do battle with a plateful of home-cooked vittles.

When Duggan Brothers abruptly closed, shortly after the nuclear meltdown, everything changed. Smiles turned to frowns. People stopped waving. Car horns went silent. Laughter was no longer heard on the playground. Sidewalks were empty, and lawns were no longer watered or mowed. It was as if in one fell swoop, the town that had meant everything to everyone, no longer meant anything to anyone.

Then the sightings began.

The first occurred in August of 1979, not long after the incident on Marathon Island, which at the time, was considered the second worst nuclear accident in the world.

Ruth Ann Grigsby reported her startling encounter after an evening stroll home from purchasing lottery tickets at the Derndoff's

Convenience store located across the street from Duggan Brothers. She only lived two short blocks from the place, so walking to and from was commonplace for her. As she left the store, she clumsily dropped one of the tickets she was loosely holding in her left hand. The ticket flittered toward the pavement, guided by a mischievous evening breeze. Letting out an audible sigh, fearing she'd lose the ticket to the wind, she lunged forward to retrieve it. Sluggish in her attempt to resume an upright position, she caught site of midnight black feet attached to the bottom half of an equally dark set of legs standing directly in front of her. There were no shoes or pants that she could determine. Startled, she dropped her ticket again and shuffled backwards, hoping to catch a full glimpse of the being who had appeared before her; however, the feet and legs were gone, as well as whatever they had been attached to.

She felt it impossible that a human being

could appear, seemingly from nowhere, only to vanish as rapidly as they had arrived. Hands shaking and her composure teetering on the brink of full panic, Mrs. Grigsby assured herself that what she had seen was merely a hallucination—a trick of the eye inspired by the eerie quiet of the night. She flattened her shirt against the sides of her torso, patted her hair-sprayed head and negotiated a direct path in the direction of her house.

Then something else happened.

With every step forward, she could hear a matching set of footsteps in sync with her own. Without hesitation, and without looking back, she ran. The purse secured around her right shoulder shimmied down her arm and fell to the ground with a thud. Her face contorted in an expression of terror, as if at any moment, her shoulder blades would be snatched from behind, and her body drug through the cold street then into the unknown.

Eyeing her lone porch light in the distance,

she frantically tried to recall if she had left the front door unlocked. Ruth Ann could feel something behind her as the audible *click-clack* of her stalker's steps grew closer. Her porch was still five paces away as tears streamed down her cheeks.

She lunged for the doorknob, falling into the quaint living room, kicking the door closed behind her with a shoeless left foot. Gasping to catch what breath she had left, she slid to her knees. Pulling the curtain of the narrow window to the side, she looked toward the road, terrified of what she might see.

There *it* stood.

A straight, slender figure, not much wider than a telephone pole, arms to its side, as if shrouded in its own shadow. It stared blankly, cold and unassuming, with no semblance of human emotion. Ruth Ann, through the fog of her rapid breath clouding the window pane, watched with a chill as the shadow figure slowly faded into the darkness.

Sinking to the floor, her back against the door, she leaned toward the small end table next to the pink floral canvas love seat, and did the only thing she knew to do.

"9-1-1—what's your emergency?" the woman on the other end of the receiver replied.

FOUR

MARATHON ISLAND

Mrs. Martinez yells into the second-floor stairwell, "Michael—food's done! And your crazy friends are at the door."

Michael, exhausted from the harrowing rubber bullet assassination attempt in Old Man Horner's woods, had slept in. Groggy, he slicks back his greasy black hair. Using his socks as skis, he slides down the steps—the smell of freshly cooking breakfast burritos guides the way.

"Smells great, Ma." He smiles.

"Thanks, mijo—door."

Michael skates across the bamboo floor, like an aggressive hockey defenseman. Standing at the glass storm door, staring at three annoyed faces, he sticks his tongue out, and swings open the door. "Sup, guys. Come on in. Ma's got breakfast burritos going."

Single file, they walk in, feeling the immediate intoxication of the aromas emanating from the kitchen.

"Mrs. M, that smells *so gooood*!" says Nia.

Mrs. Martinez leans backward away from the stove to catch a glimpse of the motley crew that just entered her hallway. "Ahh, Nia, always one with the compliments. Gracias, petardo. Now come sit down and eat."

On the table is a large, round, colorful, Mexican-art-inspired plate stacked high with medium-sized burritos stuffed with bacon, egg, cheese, and julienne-cut potatoes. The steam from the plate wafts up toward the ceiling in billowy puffs. Kyle, standing just behind Skyler, nudges her. "Looks like Marathon Island," he whispers.

"Shhh," Skyler shoots back.

"What's that, Kyle? You say something?" asks Mrs. Martinez.

"Oh, nothing. No, I uhh—hey, what are those boxes over there, Mrs. M?

Mrs. Martinez stops stirring the skillet of eggs and bacon. She turns around to face Kyle. "Those?" Sighing. "Just boxes of paperwork we've had stacked in the basement from over the years. Michael's dad collected news stories and current event clippings. There's probably stuff from the nuclear meltdown—most likely tax papers mixed in as well. He loved those old stories. After I'm done here, I'm hauling them up to the storage area in the attic."

After Mrs. Martinez turns back around, Michael looks at Nia, Kyle, and Skyler, tilting and jerking his head to the side in the direction of the boxes, hoping someone telepathically gets his hint.

"Hey, *uhh*, we can take them up for you," Kyle says.

"Yeah, no problem, Mrs. M!" says Nia.

Mrs. Martinez turns back around and looks at her son, "Michael, take notes—these amigos of yours, very helpful," she says. "Now, you four, *eat!*" Mrs. Martinez unloads the fresh batch of eggs and bacon onto the hot plate in the center of the table and shuffles off to tend to the laundry piled in the hamper by the living room sofa.

Meanwhile, four hungry mouths turn the mound of piping hot breakfast burritos into what looks more like remnants of debris from a wood chipper. Bits of bacon and strips of soft tortilla shells litter the plates. The hot-plate steam has long disappeared into the abyss of Mrs. Martinez's dining room. The fan above the stove still hums loudly, acting as white noise to the now full-bellied party of four, whispering their plans for the box transfer.

Michael leans in toward the other three,

flicking a piece of burrito with his thumb and middle finger. "Okay, look, Ma said she thinks there are papers in there from the nuclear meltdown. I say we get up to the attic and root through those boxes to see what we can find. I gotta know what's in there," whispers Mike. "My dad, he—he's always had those boxes, but I never knew where they were."

"Well, your mom's busy and seems super distracted. Now's the time," says Skyler.

"Agreed."

"*Ma*! Hey, *Ma*! We're taking those boxes up now!" Michael yells.

There is no response from Mrs. Martinez, so they each stand and walk toward the boxes, grabbing one off the stack—soon realizing they are going to have to make two trips. Each with a box in hand, they march up the stairwell to the second-floor. At the end of the upstairs hallway is a door that leads to the attic. Michael sets his box down, allowing him to turn the knob on the door. A rush of stale confined air sweeps past the group. "The attic," he says, bowing.

"I hope your mom doesn't find us rummaging through her boxes," says Nia.

"Nah, she wears headphones when she does laundry. We're good."

Michael leads the way with Kyle pulling caboose, and the four friends carefully balance their boxes while ascending the narrow, rickety steps into the cluttered attic. "Hey, don't use that step," he says, pointing. "It's brittle. My dad never fixed it. Your foot will fall right in."

The space is a prototypical, exposed-stud, A-frame attic, complete with cobwebs, old clothing trunks, odds and ends housewares, and used furniture strewn about. It's a perfect environment to perform an unofficial box autopsy.

"Here, put 'em down here. Start looking," Michael says.

Everyone has a hand in the file-box-cookie-jar, so to speak.

Sinkhole...

Lightning storm of 2000...

Fire Department decommission...

"No, no, no."

Annual donut eating contest—

"I got it!" shouts Kyle.

As the others stop searching their boxes, Kyle pulls a partially torn, weathered clipping from the mess of miscellaneous files.

"Read it, Kyle," says Skyler...

50 cents
LATE EDITION
Vol. CIX68 No. 36, 274

THE
NUCLEAR
ACCIDENT

Radiation Continues To Leak From Crippled Tower

WHITE TANKS, Pa –
Radiation leaks from
the Marathon Island
nuclear power plant
continued today,
authorities said, as
debates grew over
what was described
as the most serious
incident in this
country's history,
and whether some of
its residents should
have stayed.

Marathon Island nuclear power plant.

When a feed pump malfunctioned, the turbine
water could not remove heat from the steam generator.
When this happened, the control rods dropped into the
reactor stopping the fission process. Thus, steam
bubbles appeared in the coolant pumps. With no water
flowing to remove the heat, the fuel pellets started to
melt, resulting in the meltdown.

What followed was organized chaos. Sirens
sounded and emergency personnel were dispatched. In the
days and weeks after the accident, White Tanks became a
ghost town. Duggan Brothers Steel Mill halted operations, as hordes of residents evacuated the area.

For those that remained, telephone calls
flooded emergency dispatch centers reporting strange
appearances of

"Wait, that's it? Where's the rest?" asks Mike.

"I dunno. That's it. It's torn."

"Well maybe it's at the bottom of the box."

"I looked, man."

"*Well look harder!*"

"Hey, I—"

"Michael! What are ya'll doing up there?" shouts Mrs. Martinez.

"Ma! Boxes! We took the…we're coming down!" yells Mike.

Knowing that Mrs. Martinez doesn't like anyone scavenging in her keepsakes and storage, Kyle, Michael, Nia, and Skyler swiftly cover the open boxes with the lids and shove them against the wall, stacking them neatly beside a rocking chair. In their haste, a few papers float to the floor, but no one sticks around to gather them up.

Kyle folds the Marathon Island newspaper article into the shape of a small rectangle and slides it into his jeans pocket. He weaves his way past another rocking chair and makes a right turn, descending the attic steps to join up with the rest of his friends who are already being scolded by Mrs. Martinez for being in the attic so long.

Pulling the door closed behind him, a gust of air exposes a tiny piece of shredded newspaper that had been wedged between two envelopes containing tax returns that were callously dropped from one of the boxes. In bright, blood-red ink, scribbled across the top of the newspaper are the words:

SHADOW PEOPLE

FIVE

KYLE KETCHUM

Kyle fumbles around in his front left jeans pocket for the key to unlock Fort Bliss. "Thanks for meeting me here, Skyler."

Skyler stands with her thumbs hooked into her belt-loops, waiting for Kyle to pop the door bolt. "Not a problem. So why the secrecy this morning?"

The rickety door makes a popping sound as the bolt dislodges with Kyle catching it in mid-air.

"I couldn't sleep."

Kyle and Skyler walk through the fort's entrance, passing through a beam of sunlight shining through the moonroof.

Noticing his own shadow cast against the light on the wood floor, Kyle abruptly stops and shakes his head, as if he's knocking the fog out of his brain. "I keep having the same nightmare. Not every night. But many nights. You should maybe sit down," he says to Skyler.

Skyler wipes off the dust that's collected on her tree stump and takes a seat. "The others heard this?" she asks.

"No, no. I don't even—I don't even know if you should hear this—"

"C'mon, Kyle! You know I like this stuff."

"Yeah, but—" Kyle's hearing aid makes a high-pitched piercing sound, forcing him to grab at his left ear. He winces in pain, clutching both sides of his head, he falls to the floor.

TOWN

"What are you doing on the floor, Kyle?"

"I hate it here."

"Oh, c'mon, Kyle. The doctor's office— what's wrong with it? We've been coming here a long time now," Kyle's mom says.

Kyle slides into the chair next to her— the same way he had two years earlier during the doctor visit after his recurring nightmares had begun. "I'm only here because you don't believe me," he replies.

"It's not that I…well, I mean, look, it's *hard* to believe what you're saying is all. It's not that I don't believe you."

"You don't, though. It's okay," concedes Kyle.

The receptionist behind the check-in counter smirks at Kyle with knowing eyes, giving him an uneasy feeling.

The Langoliers & Associates Otolaryngology Center for the Deaf has been Kyle's primary care physician's office since birth. They have been treating his Meniere's disease and subsequent hearing loss with state-of-the-art hearing aids, along with revolutionary gene therapy trials, which, unfortunately, came with a bizarre side effect that no one, outside of Kyle, accepts.

"I hear things; things regular people shouldn't hear. It scares me."

"What? Having improved hearing?" His mom chuckles.

Kyle looks away from the receptionist, and turns toward his mom. "No. I'm scared of the people at this place."

Kyle's mom rests her right hand on Kyle's thigh. "Kyle, do you remember a few years ago, during the winter when Whitney was stuck in the storm-drain down at the corner of our street? You pulled the grate to the side, climbed in that dank, dark pipe, and rescued her. You did that all by yourself. Do you remember the scare you gave *me* when you weren't responding to my calls for dinner from the kitchen while you were supposed to be in the living room? I do. *That* scared me. What you did was brave. You're my brave boy. You've always been a brave, fearless boy. A leader." She paused. "To this day, I still don't know how on God's green earth you heard her meowing while you were *inside* the house."

"I told you I—"

The door to the waiting room swings open and a new doctor's assistant Kyle has never seen before glances at her clipboard and calls his name.

Kyle leans into his mom's shoulder, burying his face near her ear. "They all have pointed teeth."

Kyle stands up from the waiting room chair and walks slowly toward the smiling assistant.

Kyle's mom follows behind.

The assistant guides Kyle down the fluorescent light illuminated hallway, past the patient cubicles. They make a left turn at the water cooler and proceed to Room 5, where the assistant extends her arm as if showing him a new car he's won.

"Andddd we're here. Dr. Jenkins will be in shortly."

Before Kyle's mom can turn around and say thanks, the assistant is gone.

"Their skin is like charcoal, Judy."

"Can't you ever call me Mom?"

"I know they know that *I know*. But you don't see them, do you? I do...*I do*," he whispers. "Their white coats turn black. Blacker than the moonless night. Eyes collapse into their heads. Then the teeth."

"Too many scary movies, Kyle," Judy says.

Knock, knock

"Hey, Kyle. *Judy!* Oh, Judy, so glad you're here. Always, *always* a pleasure to see your face!" proclaims Dr. Jenkins. "And what brings you here today, Kyle? Girls chasing you again?" He laughs.

Kyle stares at his feet. "I don't want to do

the gene therapy anymore."

"You don't want to do the gene…oh c'mon, sport! Everyone here feels you're attaining much greater results with the therapy. I mean, uhh, hey, you've said it yourself, big guy. You do hear…*better*." Dr. Jenkins rolls his chair close to Kyle, leaning forward to get an up-close look at the hearing aid. He adjusts the ear piece's toggle button to the maximum setting. Judy is on the opposite side of Kyle, out-of-range from Dr. Jenkins's whisper, as he inches his mouth to just outside the outer rim of Kyle's ear canal. "*She'll never believe you, sport.*"

Kyle jerks his head back. "What did you say?"

"I was making an adjustment to your earpiece, Kyle. You might have heard a bit of an echo." Dr. Jenkins leans back and shoots a vibrant smile at Judy, who is searching through her oversized knock-off designer purse, trying to locate a folded-up article she had printed about a Finnish study documenting success stories regarding Dr. Jenkins' gene therapy treatment.

The new doctor's assistant from earlier opens the door and walks in holding an unopened box of latex gloves. She sets them on the counter and flashes a broad smile at Kyle, showcasing her sharp, menacing teeth.

Kyle's eyes dart toward his mother, hoping she'd seen, but she's still rummaging through her purse.

"Welp, nothing I can see here that would be considered…*irregular*, Kyle. It all looks good to me," exclaims Dr. Jenkins. He sits back and crosses his right leg over top of his left knee then taps the top of his glasses downward to rest on the bridge of his nose. "You still, uhh, *hearing things*, Kyle?"

"Judy, I want to go!" shouts Kyle.

"Kyle. Let the—"

"Now. I want to go *now!*"

"Dr. Jenkins, I…"

"No. Quite alright, Judy. He's having

a rough one is all." Dr. Jenkins squeezes her shoulder. "Stop at the front desk on your way out, would you?"

Judy leans in for a hug. Her back is to Kyle, allowing Dr. Jenkins eye contact with Kyle. He pats Judy's back, lowering his head so Kyle can only see the tops of his now transformed, bloodshot eyes. He smiles. His teeth—the shape of pointed daggers, are unkempt, discolored, rotted blades of ivory-stained evil.

Kyle trembles, frozen where he stands.

"Thank you again so much, Dr. Jenkins," Judy says.

Dr. Jenkins crosses his arms. "You both have an enjoyable day. And, Kyle…*see you soon.*"

Kyle pulls on his mom's hand, physically urging her pace down the hallway. They make a right turn by the water cooler, and zero in on the swinging exit door. Approaching the front desk to checkout, Kyle glances back through the square window in the now motionless swinging door. Dr. Jenkins appears in the corner near where the water cooler stands. He flashes his serrated teeth again and winks.

"I'm all set, Kyle. Let's *go*," says his mom.

Just before exiting the building, Kyle stops mid-stride with a grimace on his face. He grabs for his hearing aid on his right ear. Readjusting the toggle to set a softer volume, he hears two faint words echo distantly inside his ear.

"*Help us.*"

"Who's there?" Kyle asks.

"Kyle! Hey, Kyle!" Skyler violently tugs and pulls on Kyle's shirt, finally slapping him in the face for him to snap to.

Kyle sits up drenched in sweat. "Oh, hey, Skyler. What are you doing here?"

SIX

THE BLACK PATH

Skyler stares down at Kyle. "Get up, Kyle. Look at you! You're soaked," she says.

"How long have we been here?" asks Kyle. He balances himself on one knee then stands up, using Skyler's shoulder as a pull-up bar.

"Umm, only like fifteen minutes. It doesn't matter. Who cares about how long we've been here. What the heck just happened back there? Where *were* you?"

"Can we go?" asks Kyle.

"Yeah, but you're telling me what just

happened."

"I need something cold to drink." During his episode, bits of white foam had collected around the edges of his lips while opening and closing his jaw, making sloshing noises until all the saliva had dried up.

"We'll go to Derndoff's."

"Through the Black Path?"

"Yep."

Kyle wipes his mouth. "Well, alright. It's still daytime."

Kyle and Skyler lock up Fort Bliss and make their way out of the woods in the direction of Cedar Street toward the entrance of the place they hated to go.

The Black Path is a narrow, quarter-mile long asphalt walkway carved through a section of dense maple and sycamore trees, connecting the upper and lower elevation of White Tanks. The township originally constructed it as a single-lane access road for workers of the Duggan Brothers Steel Mill to get to and from work, but after several accidents involving cars plunging over the side during icy conditions, it was finally closed off with chain at both ends to prohibit cars from using it. After its official closing—a few years before the mill shut down—the path became a walking shortcut for anyone in the hills to make their way down to the valley where Derndoff's convenience store sits. Though as time passed, the landscape of the path had changed drastically and the nickname for the walkway was born. The weeds reclaimed what was rightly theirs, narrowing the path even further, but more important and terrifying enough, black nylon dolls filled with cotton stuffing began appearing in the tree line. They had no eyes, no hair, no clothing or facial features. They were lean, as if malnourished, and were hung with string or nailed to trees all the way down the length of the path. At times, the dolls had numbered in the hundreds, some perched high in the air where even extension ladders couldn't reach. No one knew how or why the dolls were there, or who put them there, but it forever changed the way people used the path. Walking it during the daytime hours was considered brave. Walking *The Black Path* at night was considered lunacy.

"You ready?" Skyler asks.

Kyle shrugs. "Let's just get this over with before dark."

They step over the padlocked chain at the end of Cedar Street and stare down the dimly-lit corridor of the tree canopy covered path with trepidation in their stride.

"Gosh, even when it's sunny, there's not much light in here," Kyle mumbles.

"Never is." Skyler looks to her right, studying the dolls, pinned and hung from the trees, half expecting them to move. She looks back at Kyle. "Now that I'm getting you that drink, you owe me a story."

"Yeah *I*…"

"You totally blacked out back there, Kyle! Your eyes rolled back and you were talkin' weird, like you were dreaming." Skyler looks excited, like she'd seen something that came right out of a horror movie.

"A nightmare really…"

"So, what'd you see?"

"Can we just get that drink first? My mouth is still all dusty."

"*Kyle Ketchum!*"

"I'll tell you on the way back, I promise."

Each step forward brings more black dolls into focus. The deeper down the path they walk, the denser the doll placements become. Kyle and Skyler increase their pace to the point where they are almost jogging. Neither wants to admit to the other that they started jogging first, so neither one says anything—they just keep going. Nearing the end of the path, light filters in again from the sky above where the canopy thins out. They step over the locked chain at the bottom and continue walking alongside the road toward Derndoff's.

"What cha' gonna drink?" asks Skyler.

"*Anything!* I'm dyin' here."

As they approach the automatic doors of Derndoff's, the doors don't open.

"Sensor busted?"

"I don't know. Hop up and down."

Nothing.

They both move away from the doors, thinking maybe it will reset itself. They walk backwards in the opposite direction, stepping off the entrance mat. As soon as they're clear of the mat, the doors begin sliding apart. They run toward the doors, only to be denied again by their abrupt closing.

"Seriously!?" shouts Skyler.

Inside, Kyle sees a lone cashier—an elderly woman, watching them through the window with a peculiar, tight-lipped smile on her face. Her gaze is unwavering, almost baiting them to try the door again. Kyle stands beside the doors, away from the mat, while Skyler walks backward toward the parking lot.

The doors open. Kyle jumps to his left

and holds the doors while Skyler dashes toward the opening. Kyle holds the doors open just enough that they both squeeze through. They both look at the cashier.

"What's up with the doors?" Skyler asks the cashier.

"Drinks are over there. Special today."

Kyle leans into Skyler. "How'd she know we're here for that?"

"I'm creeped out. Let's get the stuff and go."

They load their drinks onto the conveyor belt and watch them inch their way toward the cashier whose name is *Ruth Ann*–according to her nametag. She has maintained her menacingly amused expression, like a wax figure in a museum.

"Special today," she says.

"Special? *What special?* No, how much?" asks Skyler.

The elderly woman's eyebrows change direction, framing a scowl. Her eyes close and her head and neck begin to oscillate, like she's having some sort of spasm.

"Special…today," she says in a slower, deeper, baritone voice that doesn't sound like it's coming from her own vocal chords.

Kyle and Skyler jump to snatch their drinks from the conveyer belt, but Kyle's drink tips over in the commotion. He stops in his tracks, turns around to grab the bottle, and sees the old woman's eyelids fluttering in rapid motion.

They break for the doors and run as fast as they can down the street toward the opening for *The Black Path*, frequently glancing back over their shoulders to make sure the woman isn't chasing after them. They jump over the locked chain and begin their ascent back up the path. Both gasping for breath.

"Never…I never…"

Skyler, having forgotten all about Kyle's story says, "I just wanna—she gasps—go back home."

They stop about halfway up the path to

finally crack open their drinks when Kyle notices a haggard-looking note about the size of a piece of notebook paper pinned to a large maple tree.

"Skyler, look!" Kyle points to the note, then scratches his cheek. "Rag…Rag… R.A.G.? Initials? Name?"

"We need to show this to Michael and Nia." Skyler steps up to the tree and reaches out to tear the note from the bark.

Kyle grabs at his ear, doubles over and shrieks in pain.

"Oh, heck no, Kyle—not again!" screams Skyler.

"No, I got stung by a bee."

SEVEN

DETOUR

Kyle and Skyler emerge from the path to a waning summer sun wrapped delicately around what's left of scattered clouds—just enough daylight to feel comfortable, having escaped the chained border between safety and uncertainty. Skyler is holding the note they'd found on the tree. Kyle's hand holds the back of his ear, applying pressure to stop the throbbing pain radiating throughout his skull.

"I thought you were going to pass out again and start talking otherworldly," Skyler says.

"C'mon, Sky, it hurts. I mean that really hurt." Kyle manages to flash a reassuring smile at her.

Skyler pauses, furrows her brow, and the two simultaneously laugh out of pure relief, having survived the four-minute sprint of terror.

Side by side they walk further away from The Black Path and continue their hike up Monroe Street toward Essex where Nia lives.

"I hope she's home," says Kyle, looking up at the faint stars beginning to appear. He is concerned about nightfall and the contents of the note's warning.

"Where's *she* go?" snickers Skyler. "She probably sits at home and thinks up theories about how the dark side of the moon is occupied by ancient aliens who invented algebra."

"Well, it *is* difficult."

"My theory on Nia?"

"No. Algebra."

They approach the wooden swing gate entrance to Nia's front yard to the tune of the neighbor's barking terriers. At the porch door, Kyle knocks hard twice, pauses, then knocks hard twice again, alerting Nia that it's them. The door swings open and an excited Nia, wearing an "Are We Alone?" tee-shirt, high fives both Kyle and Skyler.

"Oh my gosh! You guys! I'm so glad you're here. Let me ask you…I was sitting out back thinking…what if the reason manned space missions to the moon stopped was because of aliens?"

Kyle's jaw drops.

Skyler shoots him a sideways smile. "Nia, we need to come in," she says.

"*Daaaaad*, Ky and Sky are here, going upstairs in my rooooom. Knock first."

The two girls enter Nia's room, and Kyle closes the door behind him.

Nia sits on the purple throw spread across her bed. An X-Files *I Want to Believe* poster is on the wall overhead. "So, okay! About my alien idea…"

"Nia, stop. Listen," Kyle says. "Call Michael. He needs to be here too."

Nia's phone is on her nightstand next to an orange lava lamp. She picks up the phone without hesitation and connects with Michael. *"Yeah, right now! I'll watch for you out the window. Bye!"*

She hangs up the phone and looks at Kyle and Skyler. "You saw something, didn't you—I knew it!"

Skyler sinks her hand inside of her pocket, unfolds the note from the tree, and flings it into Nia's lap.

Nia turns the upside-down note and reads it aloud in an audible whisper.

"That's not the only thing," says Skyler. "Derndoff's…something creepy is going on there. We went to get drinks, the doors wouldn't open, we had to do all of this crazy stuff to get it to open, no one's inside, this old lady I've never seen before is like convulsing, and repeating her words..."

"Pretty much, we ran," says Kyle. "We ran like Olympians back up the path."

"*Oooooooooooh*...the path," Nia repeats.

A pebble hits the top of Nia's bedroom window. "Mike! Come on up. Door's open. Dad's asleep."

"Cool."

Michael enters the room and sees that they're sitting in a circle on the floor like they're having a séance. "I...guess I forgot... *the candles?*" he says, laughing. He looks at Kyle. "Hey, your ear's all swelled up."

"Bee."

"You got stung by a bee!?" Nia shrieks.

Michael joins his friends on an area rug with a solar system design spread across the hardwood floor. He pushes his finger onto Skyler's forehead. "Sup." He looks at Kyle. "So, what's this all about?"

Kyle points at the note that is now lying on

the carpet. Michael picks it up. "RAG? Who's RAG? Or is that like, R.A.G., like initials?"

"That's just it. We don't know," says Skyler. "When's the last time you were at Derndoff's, Mike? Seen that old lady in there?"

"What old lady?"

"The *only* one that's old."

"There's no old lady in there. Shifty's mom works in there, and the two brothers that stock the shelves, sometimes they're on register. That's who I always see."

Kyle is quiet. The white noise of the murmured speculations lulls him into having an epiphany. Staring down at his shoes, he snaps to, and looks at Skyler. "She had a nametag."

"So?"

Kyle reaches over Michael to grab the note, holds it up, and points to the signature, "R.A.G." His mind flashes to the nametag on her uniform that said *Ruth Ann*.

"*Grigsby!?*" shouts Nia.

"No, no way. That lady that went missing

way back?" says Skyler. "They never found her."

Kyle turns to face Skyler. "Maybe *we* did."

Michael grabs the note from Kyle and glances at the words again. "If that's a warning, right? Maybe it's not. Maybe it's a signal or code or something. Maybe she's out there at night, and she needs to tell you all something. I dunno."

"You know, I was perfectly fine sitting here thinking about the moon and space and aliens!" says Nia.

"You wanna do a manned mission of our own, Nia?" asks Skyler.

"To where?"

Kyle stands up and walks over to the bedroom window, looking up at the moon. "*The Black Path.*"

"No, no, no," says Nia. "I'm not going anywhere near Derndoff's *now.*"

Kyle turns back around from the window and looks at Nia. "Who said anything about

Derndoff's?"

Skyler looks at Nia and shrugs.

"I know where you're thinking, Kyle," says Michael. "The very bottom of the path has that—"

"Detour," Kyle finishes the thought.

EIGHT

NIA PARK

"Nia, c'mon, nighttime's not so bad. You have us," says Michael, walking over to the light switch on the wall, his expression mischievous. "Besides, it's not that scary. Look, I'll show you."

Michael clicks his fingers and points to Kyle, gesturing for him to pull down the window shade and close the curtains.

Skyler turns to Michael. "I don't think you should…"

"Mike, don't!" cries Nia. "I hate the dark!

It makes…"

"Shhhh, s'okay," he whispers, flicking the switch on a green, glow-in-the-dark faceplate. "See, Nia…nothing."

The room is pitch black with only a tiny sliver of orange street lamp light peeking through the side curtain. Kyle and Michael are goofing around, waving a hand in front of their face, trying to glimpse the silhouette. Skyler is concerned for Nia and pats the floor erratically, like a pantomime trying to locate her voice.

"Nia, get up. We have to go."

Nia stirs on the floor, wriggling around, like a freshly unearthed nightcrawler.

"Nia, you've got to get up. We *have* to leave…*now*."

Skyler stands up, yawns, and shakes her head, causing her braid clips to rattle. She grabs her overnight bag, sensing urgency. "Thanks, Mr. Park. If ya'll need anything, let me know."

"Yes, okay, very good. Thank you, Skyler, for staying." Mr. Park removes the blanket from Nia's body and grabs her arm to pull her from sleep.

Nia is groggy. "But, Daddy, I'm scared," she says.

"I'm scared too, firecracker, but when they call, we go."

Seatbelts snap into both sockets of the base, and their beige minivan pulls away from the curb. Nia's dad reaches across the gear shifter and lays his hand on Nia's leg. "How was your sleep, little flower? Did you see the light again?"

At the age of five, Nia had developed a rare retinal condition where the visual pigment, Scotopsin, was found in her eyes, which allowed her to see in the dark, as well as being able to see ultraviolet light. Doctors were baffled at how a human could develop this animalistic trait. Nia's parents suspected the mutation might have occurred due to her exposure to trace amounts of radiation carried over from the Marathon Island accident.

"No, Daddy. Not last night. I kept the window blind open. I dreamt of Mom, though."

Mr. Park sighs. "Well, flower, you tell her all about the dream when we get to her room, okay?"

A small tear forms at the base of Nia's eye and trickles down her cheek, into the waiting hand of her dad. "Don't cry, flower. Your mom wants to see that golden smile of yours. It makes her feel happy."

Their minivan pulls into the visitor parking lot of the Building B Cancer Care Center at Community General. They exit the van holding hands, and look up at the 8th floor, where a bright purple iris flower rests in the window.

"Such a bloom," says Mr. Park, forcing a smile.

Nia slowly opens the door to her mom's

room, and pops her head in. "Mommy," she says softly.

Nia's mom, though extremely weak, raises her hand, signaling for her to come to her bedside.

Nia's dad slips back into the hallway to speak with the doctors.

"Nia," her mom whispers. "Your iris in the window is so pretty…like you. I look at it all the time, my little flower."

"Mommy, are you coming home soon?"

"I dreamt of you last night, little flower." She cracks a tiny smile. "You were always so good at seeing the light, Nia. Your eyes. Your pretty eyes could always see the light." Nia's mom turns away, looking at the iris on the windowsill. "But now you must see *in the dark.*" She turns back to look at Nia. "Your gift, my flower. Use your gift to see in the dark. In my dream, you were shown the path."

Nia cries into her mom's hand. "Shhh, no. Don't be sad. You must share joy and be my firecracker to the world. You're my firecracker in the shadowy world."

Nia's dad stands behind her and places his hands on Nia's shoulders. "Daddy, what's happening?"

"Medicine, Nia. She's just very tired. Not awake. She's very tired. Medicine makes her say things sometime." He sighs.

"Will I talk to her again, Daddy?"

"Michael, turn the light on!" yells Skyler.

"Alright, alright, geez. Her crying was starting to freak me out anyways. Why's she crying?"

Michael flips the switch and a groggy Nia uncurls herself from a blanketed fetal position in the corner of the room. "What are you guys doing here?" she asks softly, staring at her three friends like they have skittles flowing out of their noses.

Skyler shakes her head in disbelief and

removes the blanket from Nia. "Nia, we have to go."

"Huh?" says a confused Michael.

A wobbly Nia balances herself to her feet. "No. Wait. I…I should be the light. *I* must be the light. My mom says the path will be shown and I will be the light."

"I *just* turned *on* the light," says Michael.

"No, I'm the light. We'll do what you said, and we'll go down *The Black Path*, and I'll be the light," Nia exclaims. "I'm her firecracker in this shadowy world."

"Whose world?"

"Hers." Nia points to the purple iris flower that sits on her computer desk.

NINE

STELE

Toeing the asphalt boundary between safety and vulnerability, three flashlight beams cut through the nocturnal air, illuminating silhouettes of the mysteriously placed dolls flanking both sides of the coal-black asphalt. It's unusually cold out. Carbon dioxide vapers dance erratically on escape from nervous mouths. A fourth flashlight clicks on.

"*I am* the light," says Nia.

But no one moves. The funnels of light remain still, cutting into the abyss.

During a sudden rush of anxious energy, Michael hops up and down in place. "We're doing this!?"

With unified motion, eight shoes march across the safe, street-light illuminated pavement into the void. Michael's flashlight darts left then right, casting wide shadows from the doll bodies, making them appear to change direction, as if hiding from the light. "They're moving; I swear they're moving!" Michael loudly whispers.

"Not moving," says Skyler. "It's your light. See." She points her flashlight high into a tree, revealing a stationary doll's body.

"*I am* the light," says Nia in a disembodied voice.

Michael turns to Kyle. "I wish she'd stop saying that. She's been freaking me out since we left her house, bro."

Kyle shoots Michael a wry smile and watches his mouth moving, not knowing what he's saying. He had turned his hearing aid volume down prior to entering *The Black Path* to avoid hearing any startling sounds.

"When I was eight, my parents had a fight, an awful one," says Skyler. She's alert to Michael's uneasiness and attempts to distract him. "My dad put his hands on my mom. First they were yellin'—not too bad. I was under the kitchen table playin' solitaire. I heard her scream. Never heard that before, not like that. Then he stormed out, but not before shattering the kitchen window with his fist. I just sat there—glass falling to the floor, bouncing around, clicking and clanging, glass pieces covering my cards. He didn't even know I was under the table. I wasn't scared, though—nah. I knew he had a temper. All I was worried about was my mom. And was she hurt?"

"Was she okay?" asks Michael.

"When I got to her room, the bed was lying on top of her. I could see her head sticking out. He had flipped the bed and pinned her to the floor. She was having trouble breathing, so I snapped into action. All she said was—"

The leaves on the trees shuffle, a thud sound follows. A doll lies at their feet. No eyes, no nose, just pointy teeth drawn in white chalk.

"Oh, c'mon!" says Michael.

Thud. Another doll falls. *Thud.* Another. No one's moving. *Thud, thud, thud.* Several more crash through the leaves. They point their lights at each fallen doll, revealing the same, chalky white, pointy teeth. Kyle adjusts his earpiece, increasing the volume.

"*Run!*"

Dolls begin falling all around them, smacking into their shoulders, ricocheting off their heads and bouncing off the ground. It's as if an earthquake is shaking the dolls loose from their perches high in the trees, though the ground isn't shaking. Flashlight beams bob up and down with each running step of their feet.

"I think I can see the chain gate!" Kyle yells, breathing heavily. *Thud, thud, thud.*

Michael is reciting a prayer aloud. "Hail Mary full of grace…"

They jump over the chain gate.

The dolls stop falling.

Silence.

Bent over, hands on their knees, they catch their breath far enough away from the canopy in *The Black Path* to feel as if they'd escaped. They shine their lights at the path across the chain link boundary and see piles of black dolls with chalk-white pointy teeth all aimed in their direction.

"That just happen?" says Michael, breathing deeply. His hand is on his waist, he looks to Skyler. "So, what'd your mom say to you? Back there—you said she said something."

"*…don't be afraid.*"

Nia points her finger toward the fork in the road. "That's Derndoff's. Over there is—"

"The cemetery," says Kyle. "That's where we're going."

"Nope. Not after that," exclaims Michael,

pointing back to The Black Path.

Nia grabs Michael's hand. "*I am* the light."

"I swear, you gotta stop…"

"*Shh*. Look. Out there," whispers Kyle. "Yellow. Whole bunch. Looks like eyes."

"Owls?"

"Don't think so."

Reluctantly, they walk in the direction of the gravesite. No cars pass by. As they walk, the ground beneath them changes from pavement to grass. Just ahead, they see a rusted, iron swing gate with the words "White Tanks Cemetery" welded into the arch of the iron grating. A gust of wind rushes through. The weathered sign hanging below the woven words swings from side to side. The grounds are neglected, much like the rest of the town. Tufts of wild crab grass weave in and out of the round, brass grave markers. This is the part of the cemetery locals call *Land of The Living* because the plots and markers are relatively new. Chirping crickets, croaking frogs, and several hoots from owls contribute to a cacophony of twilight sounds. Ironically, the place is teaming with restless life.

"Well, this is cool and all—grave markers, old stuff…grass," says Michael.

"That's not where we're going," says Kyle. "We go to the edge, Mike. Where the stele stands."

"The what?"

"*STEE-lee.* The grave monuments, Mike. That's what they called them back then. The stele marks the boundary between the old and new cemetery." Kyle points beyond the furthest line of brass grave markers toward the yellow glow in the forgotten woods, picking up his pace to catch up with the girls.

"Man, I dunno. I just don't think it's a cool idea to—"

Kyle, Nia, and Skyler abruptly stop.

Michael trails behind. "Why'd you stop?"

No answer.

"*Hey*, guys—why'd you stop?!"

Kyle whispers to Skyler and Nia. "Have

you ever seen anything like this?"

"See what?" Michael asks, catching up.

Kyle points to four small, dilapidated gravestones at the edge of the cemetery grass with hand carved names. His head slowly turns to meet Michael's curious gaze.

"It's our names."

TEN

BLACK BREEZE

The crescent moon is at its pinnacle on the horizon, draping its light over the starry sky, like a night watchman overseeing his perimeter. The glow from the waning crescent is the cemetery's only source of natural light. A reflection in a puddle shows the faint expressions of dumbfounded faces. The flashlights aren't budging. They are fixated on the broken stone nameplates of the decrepit grave markers displaying their perfectly spelled names.

They look newly etched into an otherwise crumbling façade. Nia reaches into her pocket, anxiously searching for her phone. "Did you guys bring yours?" she asks, as she grips the device, pulling it toward her face.

The others fumble around in their pants, each grabbing their phones.

"Who are we calling?" asks Michael.

"*Pictures!*" whispers Nia loudly.

"Hmm..."—flash—"my screen's all weird." Flash. "I can't get the...*why* is it all blurry!?" Flash. "Ughhh! Kyle, try yours."

Flash. Kyle turns his phone around and shows Nia. "See, fuzzy." Flash. "Mine's got like, static on it, like a broken T.V." Flash. "Skyler?"

Flash. She shows her phone to the group. "S'messed up."

Michael flips his phone in the air, letting it land on the thick grass below. "Well *now* who's gonna believe us!?"

"Yeah," says Skyler. "Buncha crazy kids tellin' people our names are on gravestones at the WTC."

Michael bends to a knee and wraps his arms around the rectangular stone with his name on it, attempting to lift it. "Can't *be*... *that*...heavy," he says, straining.

Kyle shakes his head and tries taking another picture. Flash. "Nope. Everything is screwed up and blurry." He puts the phone into his back pocket and stares at the moon. "Got any ideas?" he asks sarcastically. He turns back to Michael who is still attempting to pry the stone from the grip of the ground. "Mike, c'mon, what'd you think, we're all carrying big gravestones home? Stop it. They're like 200 pounds probably."

Skyler stands on the border where the cemetery grass ends and the dense woods begin, gazing into the cavernous entrance. Beyond this point, the gravestones are undated and the brush is overgrown. The trees grow imposingly, creating a canopy, like an oversized coffin.

"I feel claustrophobic just looking in there," Michael says.

Nia smiles wide. "It's haunted. I know it. Everyone in town who's dared to cross this boundary has said so."

"Super reassuring. I'm definitely on board now," Michael says.

"I see something in there," Skyler says. She shines her light down the tree-lined path. "Back in there, way back."

The others gather beside her in a horizontal line, peering in the direction her flashlight beam that's being swallowed by the darkness.

"I don't see anything," says Nia.

"I don't see anything either," says Michael.

Kyle lets out a sigh. "I see it," he says, looking at Skyler. "Mike, give me that note in your pocket."

Michael removes the folded note and hands it to Kyle.

Kyle unfolds the note and holds it up to the group. "Looks like this," he nods toward the beam of light. "I'll bet it's the same thing Sky and I found in *The Black Path* earlier," he says, shaking the note.

Skyler lifts her foot to take a step into the wood.

Michael pulls her back. "Wait. *Just wait*," he says. "We shouldn't be going in there. We don't know what's in there. You heard the stories. You heard 'em. My butt ain't goin' in there."

"Well then, Mikey, *you* stay here and… stand guard or something, I dunno. But we're going in." He points to the grave markers that have their names on it. "You don't want to know what *that* is?" his voice trembles.

"Well, okay, but…"

"*I am* the light," says Nia.

"Dude! She's gotta stop saying that!"

All four flashlights point in the direction of the mysterious object Skyler and Kyle can see. In one fluid, calculated motion, they uniformly step out beyond the grass line and crunch down on patches of broken twigs.

The wind stops blowing. The twilight noises fall silent.

The crickets aren't chirping, the frogs aren't bellowing, and the owls stop hooting. Nothing peeps. The air is calm. Not a single leaf is shaking. The only sounds are those of the branches crunching below their feet, and the nervous breaths escaping their mouths. They walk timidly, one cautious heel in front of each toe, avoiding as much brushwood as possible to minimize their raucous presence.

"What are we looking for exactly? Couldn't we come back during the day? And what are we supposed to do if we *do* find something? Maybe we *should* have used the phones to call someone rather than taking a bunch of fuzzy photos. I wish I'd eaten another slice of pizza at dinner. Might have been my last meal." Michael's barrage is a side effect of his jumpiness.

"*Shh.* Right there." Kyle and Skyler point their lights just ahead, twenty paces up.

Michael snaps his head to the left and

shines his light at a tall, wide tree. "I just saw something!"

"*Shh*, no, it's right up here."

"No, I'm tellin' you." He darts his head to the right this time, in the direction of another large tree, dropping his flashlight. "See, *look*, I'm tellin' you there's a—"

Skyler and Kyle reach the tree that they had seen from a distance. Kyle unfolds the note he has in his hand and holds it up to where another note is pinned. He shines his light at the two notes, comparing both samples. "Same paper. Same everything." He directs the light to the bottom of the note and turns to look at Skyler. "Same initials."

Michael bends down, picking up his flashlight, murmuring frustration over his friends ignoring him. He is ten steps away from giving them a piece of his mind, when suddenly his light illuminates the entrance to the path they'd just traveled. He drops his flashlight again and begins to stumble backward, trying to shout the names of his friends, but all he can push out are faint murmurs.

"Nnnniii…K-k-kyy…"

"Mikey, what? All night long with the…" Skyler turns away from tree with the pinned note and sees Michael stumbling backward. "Why the heck you walkin' backwards like that?"

"*TURN… AROUND!*" he yells.

ELEVEN

MICHAEL MARTINEZ

Michael is groggy. He opens his eyes and peers up at an oddly aligned group of stars through a small opening in the tree tops. There are bits of soggy dirt on the edges of his mouth and shirt. *It looks like an arrow*, brushing the debris off his face. "Kyle…Skyler, did you see it?" Still in a daze, Michael rocks himself up to a sitting position. Clumps of dirt fall from the back of his thick, black hair onto the ground. He stares at the fallen flashlight. The beam is still shining bright, illuminating a translucent fog rising from the earth. "Nia, you saw them, right? You guys saw them, *right?*" He turns toward the tree where they'd all been standing, and realizes no one is there. The note is gone too.

It's eerily silent. Michael stands, struggling to cup his hands around his mouth to yell out into the woods. "*Kyyyyyle! Skyyyyler! Niaaaaa!*" His arms feel like weighted steel rods with anvils for hands. He can't figure out why his upper body is so tired. He gazes up at the sky and locates the abnormally placed starry arrow. It's pointing in the direction of where they initially entered the woods.

"Won't find them," says a man's voice.

Startled, Michael jerks his head toward the entrance where the voice echoed. "Who're you?"

An obscurely tall, slender man with a craggy, weathered nose, sunken cheekbones, and thin mouth is standing at the arched entry to the old woods. He's wearing a buttoned white lab coat with a nametag attached to the pocket, overtop a paisley-blue tie, pleated khaki pants, and shiny black boots on his feet. Atop his head is a white hard hat with an M.I. logo emblazoned on the front. In his right hand, he's holding architect paper snapped to a clipboard. "*Oh,*" he says. "Martin, I guess. You can call me Martin."

Confused, Michael proceeds with caution, stepping closer to where the man is standing. "Martin huh? So, where'd you come from then…*Martin*? And where's my friends?"

The man smirks, and makes a fist. Sticking his thumb out, he points behind his left shoulder, all while maintaining a sharp focus on Michael. "Out there."

Michael looks out, and to his wonderment, sees two large nuclear towers in the cemetery, billowing steam into the night sky. He's having trouble believing what his eyes are seeing. He pinches his arm to be sure. His suspicion of what's happening becomes clearer by the second. "Is this real or am I projecting?"

"What's real? Who determines what's real? I am real, but perhaps *you are not*," Martin says with a wry smile. "Perhaps your astral body—"

"I asked about my friends."

"Yes…*yes* your friends. Your friends are fine…*for now*. Though, I wouldn't wait too long to tell them the way out."

"The way out?"

"*Yesssss*," he hisses. "The way out. *They* don't take pity on children just because they're young. *They* don't take pity on anyone, really. *They* don't care."

"They?"

"The black breeze—the ones with no faces." Martin forces a wide, clenched-teeth smile, points to his mouth and speaks through a locked jaw. "The ones with the teeth."

"I feel like I've seen you somewhere." Michael turns around, squinting his eyes toward the depths of the woods. "I've been here before."

Martin is loosely holding the clipboard face-up in an open palm, and Michael notices. On it is an intricate drawing of four nuclear steam towers. Two of the towers have fire spewing from the base. There are crudely drawn people running frantically in all directions, pouring out of the building. On a red bench near the building's exit door, a defeated man in a white lab coat is sitting with his legs crossed, watching the chaos unfold around him.

"Did you get a good look?"

"*Is that your—*"

"You already know the answer, Michael. You were there that day. I saw the boy with black hair, hovering like a hummingbird. You remembered what you saw, yet you chose to ignore it."

"You let those people die," Michael said accusingly.

Martin sighs. His fingers relax, involuntarily dropping the clipboard to the ground. The whites of his eyes fill the sockets as they roll back, like a great white shark before a fatal strike. His eyelids begin fluttering. He turns to face the nuclear towers that have appeared in the cemetery, methodically removing the white lab coat, one sleeve at a time, slowly revealing a bare arm covered in blackened ash that no longer resembles anything human. The white hard hat that fit snugly on his head slinks off and falls to the ground. With his back to Michael, he walks toward the steam towers.

"They *become* you," he whispers.

Michael watches in horror as Martin stumbles toward the nuclear towers with erratic motions, as if the bones in his legs have been dislocated. With each step, another inch of lab coat peels from his body, exposing more charcoaled flesh.

Before Michael can witness the final transformation of what Martin is morphing into, he staggers backward, tripping over the now dimmed flashlight.

"I think he fainted! Mike! Hey, Mike!"

"Get him up!"

"Grab his arms. You, that side. *Pull!*"

Skyler furiously slaps the side of Michael's face to wake him up. "Boy, git' up!"

At the entrance of the woods, the winds swirl, like ghostly tap dancers through the brittle leaves, revealing what Michael had alerted them to. "*Git...*up!" yells Skyler.

Drowsy, and barely awake, Michael blinks repeatedly, trying to focus on his surroundings while being held up by his friends. Facing the tree canopy, he glimpses a starry arrow pointing toward the deep woods.

"Which way do we go!?" shrieks Nia.

"This way, I think!" screams Kyle.

"No," Michael mumbles. "We go that way." He points, directing his crew to a path alongside a row of overturned gravestones.

Kyle leans over Michael's upside-down face. "How do you know?"

Michael whispers, "I saw them die."

TWELVE

EIGHT EYES

The churning winds at the mouth of the woods turn black. Michael's body weighs heavy in the arms of Kyle and Skyler, who nervously peer into the remaining cemetery light, slowly being eclipsed by the movement of the shadows.

"The darkness is growing," whispers Michael, as he shakes off his remaining stupor.

"Who was dead?" asks Kyle.

Michael wipes his face from his forehead to his chin. "Look in front of you, Kyle. Look what's happening *right* in front of you."

"How do you know where we go?"

"Okay. Three nights ago, you…*you* wore those camo pants your mom told you to throw out. You wore 'em to bed, okay…the Eagles jersey you had on, your fish tank light burned out. You were reading a pamphlet on cochlear implant surgery. Your hearing aid was on your nightstand. Your mom came up to your room. You called her Judy."

Kyle raises his eyebrows. Michael's accuracy is astonishing.

"You asked her for a new bulb for the tank: 60 watts."

"How did you—"

"I was on the ceiling—"

"Listen to that," says Nia. The stir in the woods re-awakens its nocturnal creatures, each louder than the next. It's as though they can sense the impending danger coming for them and are trying to warn the group. *"They know."*

Near the entrance, slender, humanoid-looking shapes gradually emerge from the blowing, black winds, and drip down in ethereal liquid from the affected tree branches, like calcium carbonite forming a stalactite.

"Look at that!"

Hundreds of "ribbit, ribbit, ribbit" croaks bounce off the tree trunks, and smash into Kyle's sensitive hearing aid, forcing him to reach for the volume, causing Michael to fall.

"Do you *see* what's happening?" he says, lying on the ground.

"I can't move."

"Me neither."

"I can't either."

Frozen in fear by what's materializing at the entrance, Kyle communicates instructions to Nia, but his mouth moves without sound.

"I don't know what you're saying!"

"Ribbit, Ribbit, Ribbit…" The frogs are deafening, rattling their ear drums, spinning the acoustics into words of caution.

"Rubbit, Rubbit, *Run-it*."

"They're saying run-it?"

A jarring thunder of croaks envelop the woods. "Run-it, Run-it, Run…"

"You hear them!?" Michael shouts. "It sounds like they're saying…"

Nia tears the note from the tree.

Michael leaps to his feet, and they stare at the entrance—more specifically, what's staring back. They can hardly believe what they're seeing.

Shadowmen.

"…run-it…run-it…run-it…"

There are no eyes, no noses, no facial features that resemble anything living, just a thin slit for a mouth. Their blackened bodies are lean like the emaciated dolls from The Black Path, with slim arms, punctuated by spindly, needled fingers.

"Eight eyes!" exclaims Nia.

"They don't have eyes," whispers Michael.

"*Us.* Not them. It's the first time we've all seen them while we're together." She blinks hard and opens her eyes again. "They're real."

Skyler looks at Nia and points to her shirt. "We're *not* alone," she concedes.

"...when black breeze blows...they become you..." mumbles Nia, reading from the note in her hand.

One of the figures raises its arm, pointing an elongated, twig-thin finger in the direction of the group, while another brings a finger to its mouth, mimicking a "Shh" gesture.

"What's it doing? Kyle, *what's it doing?*"

"I dunno."

The slits of their mouths open, revealing a gaping maw with long, jagged, red-tinted teeth, as if freshly consumed victims had just fallen prey to their unsympathetic hunger. Their heads begin to shake violently, reverberating from side to side, oscillating in place with blurring speed.

"That's like at Derndoff's when the..."

"I'm not gettin' a good feelin'," says Skyler.

Chunks of red debris spew from their mouths, smacking the tree trunks with a crackle.

"I think we should—"

The frogs erupt into an amphibious chorus. "Run...rib...run. Run...rib...run."

"*Run!*" screams Kyle.

Time slows. Everything slackens to a halt. They run, but the motion feels like their bodies are underwater in a dream they can't wake up from. Crooked expressions of panic exaggerate their faces. Frantic, they turn around, just enough to see where the shadowmen are.

Realizing they've forgotten the flashlight, Kyle stops. He harkens back to a memory from Derndoff's when he tipped the drink over on the conveyor belt. *I must get it*, he tells himself. They're close. The shadows glide along the earthen floor with effortless motion; their black winds tail behind, like rogue comets, decimating the tree leaves left in their wake. They're heading for Kyle. Kyle seizes the flashlight, but not before a gangling, black arm

105

reaches out, touching his leg, narrowly missing a full grab. "Ouch!" he screams, pointing the flashlight at the head of the figure. It whooshes away, retreating as if it has been hurt.

"Guys, wait!" Kyle yells, hobbling. He's running faster than he ever has in his life just to catch up.

With the girls in front of him, and Kyle still behind, Michael looks up into the night sky and sees the starry arrow pointing to the fallen gravestones ahead.

"Right!" he shouts, as they negotiate the hairpin turn down the withered path.

The air is thick—blanketed by an overpowering stench of putrefied death. Cacophonic sounds of swirling winds shearing off tree branches echo behind them. The croaking frogs fade from ear shot.

"Are you sure—gasp—this is the way?" shouts Skyler.

"It connects to—gasp—Old Man Horner's." Michael grabs at his side. "We never—gasp—used that path."

Kyle is shaking the flashlight as it flickers off and on. He continues to point it in the direction of where the winds are howling. "Stupid thing…*work!*" The light continues flickering, staying off longer than it stays on.

"Just up there!" Michael yells. "We're crossing into Horner's!"

"They're right behind me!" screams Kyle, running with the flashlight pointing over his shoulder. The burning sensation on his calf intensifies as a blackened finger reaches out for his leg.

Nia and Skyler approach the opening in the path just before reaching Horner's woods and can see Michael and Kyle running through tree branches as the flashlight bobs up and down.

"Where are you going!?" asks Skyler.

"They need me!" yells Nia, her voice disappears into the woods.

The light burns out.

Kyle runs faster, crying, waiting for sinister hands to tug on his shoulders and pull him into the woods.

"*No!*" Michael screams, closing his eyes.

It's silent.

The winds stop.

"I told you…"

A bright light illuminates the cemetery woods like a football stadium. It's brighter than any light Michael and Kyle have ever seen. Both boys are lying on their stomachs, staring up at Nia in bewilderment. She's holding the flashlight.

"…*I am* the light."

Michael smiles, and the boys drop their heads to the ground in relief.

THIRTEEN

A SHOT IN THE DARK

"Orange glow!" Nia says, parting two tree branches. "That's Horner's house."

Michael stands beside Nia, helping to hold a branch. "Looks like he's got a fire going."

"Nah, that ain't him," says Skyler. "That old booze hound ain't awake." Skyler scampers to the next set of trees and pushes branches aside. "That's his neighbor."

"Lemme see," says Kyle. He walks over to Skyler. "That's a fire. It's definitely Horner's property. I'd bet on it."

"Why you limpin'?" asks Skyler.

"It's uh…"

"Bro, what's that stuff on your leg?" Michael scurries through the brush to get to Kyle and Skyler. "It looks burnt…*no*… charred."

"It is, I guess. I mean, I dunno." Kyle looks at his calf and lightly touches it, wincing. "It got me…touched me…back there when I was getting the flashlight."

The others kneel to get a good look. "It's black, like charcoal."

"What got you? Those things!? It definitely looks like charcoal," says Nia. "Does it hurt?"

"Stings."

"*WHO'S THERE! HEY!*" a gruffly voice calls out from a distance. "*WHO IS BACK THERE! I KNOW YOU'RE OUT THERE!*"

"Shhh. Shhh. Stay low. Quiet," whispers Skyler. They let go of the branches, and cover their mouths.

"Told you—it's Horner!" whispers Nia through a cupped hand.

"*NOT TONIGHT! NO, YOU'RE NOT GETTIN' ME TONIGHT. NO, NO, NO!*"

Bang! Bang!

Shots ring out.

Another!

Bang!

"He's shooting again!" Michael whispers loudly.

Whizz! Whizz! Rubber bullets cut through the leaves, like arrows lancing paper.

"*GO BACK TO THE CEMETERY WHERE YOUZ BELONG!*" yells the man.

"We gotta move—move now!! We're fish in a barrel!" Michael hisses.

Whizz! Zip!

Kyle, Skyler, and Nia dash blindly through the brush in the direction of the gun blasts.

"Wait! We're going *toward* the gun?" says Michael, in panic. "Why are we running *toward the gun?*"

111

"Throw your hands up and scream!" says Skyler. "And zig-zag!" She cups her hands to her mouth. "Hey! "Hey mister!" *Whizz! Zip! Zip!* "Stop shooting! We're just kids! We're just kids!" *Whizz! Zip!*

"STOP HARRASSING ME!" YOU CAN'T TAKE ME! YOUUUUU CAN'T TAKE ME! LEAVE ME ALONE!"

Two more shots ring out. *Bang! Bang!*

The tree limbs rustle and the group emerges from the edge of the woods with their hands up, like perpetrators caught by cops. "We—gasp—told you, we're just—gasp—kids," says Skyler.

An older man with dark overalls, a mesh trucker hat, and a long, scruffy, dark beard stands in the grass with a gun drawn. "What are you doing in *my* woods this time of night?! What are you doing in *my* woods, period?!" the man snarls.

"We…we just—gasp—got lost—gasp—is all," says Skyler.

"Lost ay?" He looks skeptical. He rests his gun against his waist and spits. "They follow you?" Nodding his head toward the woods.

"Who follow us?"

"*Them*, SKYLER. Just tell him already," says Kyle.

"Why you hobblin', boy? What's wrong wit' yer leg?" The man cocks his head to the side to get a glance. "Shadowmen. That's who I'm chasin' away. That's why the shootin'. I thought you was them," he says, spitting. He points his thumb behind his shoulder at the crackling fire. "Fire...light...heat—don't matter. They hate it." He walks over to a chair and sits. "Sit down. Let's have a look at that leg. But stay close to the fire," he says, winking.

"Thank you, Mr. Horner, I wante—"

"*How do you know my name?*"

"Everyone kno—"

"Well, that ain't my last name. It's my birth name, so don't go puttin' no mister in front of it. You kids are out awful late, I reckon. Ain't smart," he says, reaching for Kyle's calf. "They touch ya, did they?"

"Yes, sir."

"Mm. Yeah...yeah..." he mumbles, shaking his head. "I s'pose you kids wanna know what happened, do ya? Why youz in them woods and what not...snoopin' around." Horner lurches forward in his chair, inching closer to the fire. "Marathon Island, mmhmm, was a wonderful place once...suitable place. Lots of money went through there. Lots of happiness. New houses. Pretty things. Nothing like the ruin that you see today," he says, spitting into the fire. "I had a brother once— ran the place. Sister too. Both worked there. She was a technician, somethin' or other. She helped in the control room. He was the chief engineer—*the* guy who ran things—a hot-head. Mmhmm. Him or the highway. That was his temper. That's how older brothers are."

"You said *had* a brother," Michael says.

"That's right, boy. *Had.* Went missin'.

Disappeared. Gone. Vanished. Went into hiding we think."

"Why?"

"Was his fault. Whole thing. The meltdown. Many people died."

Nia's jaw drops.

"Maybe it was guilt. I'm sure it was guilt. Inspectors came when they could. They tried containing the radiation, as best they could. The fuel rods overheated. Boom. That was it. Town went mad. Things got strange. People gone missin'. Radiation sickness spread for miles. Folks saw things." Horner eased back into his chair away from the fire. "Haven't seen him since. Sister neither."

"What happened to your sister?"

"Gone, boy—ain't you listenin'? She lived near the store at the bottom of that path. I don't know. I don't go down that-a-ways for a long time—*long, long time*. Last I seen her was there, oh, many moons ago." Horner spits, the leftovers drip down his chin. "Police came to her house, phone was off the hook. That's all I know. Her shoes was on the floor, and the door was near flung wide open. Ehhh," he mumbles. "No trace." He stands up. "It don't matter. What matters is them things out there," he says, nodding to the woods. "They don't stop comin'. They're takin' everybody. They done got my sister. They done got Martin too," he says, pointing to the fire. "But if youz got the light, youz alright."

"*Kyle what time is it!?*" asks Nia.

"11:35." Kyle jumps up. "11:35! We gotta go! Our parents find out, they're gonna—"

"Wait, what'd you say?" asks Michael, looking at Horner.

"What, boy?" Horner replies, staring at the fire.

"You said a name."

"I did so," he says, snickering. "That's a big part to leave out of a story, ain't it?" He sarcastically laughs. "My brother's name was Martin."

Michael stands up from his chair like his pants caught fire.

"Why, boy…you done shot out your chair like you know him."

"No, I…*I*…"

"Mike, you good?" asks Nia. "*Mike.*"

"Yeah…yeah…I—"

"C'mon, we gotta go…*now!*" pleads Kyle. "Mr. Horner, it…it was nice to talk with you but…"

"You stay outta them woods now," Horner says, extending his soot-black hand. The others stand up from their chairs and give him a cautionary shake.

Michael is dazed, and walks past Horner without shaking his hand.

The crew exits the yard and begins walking up Cedar Street for home.

Horner wryly smiles, throws his rubber bullet gun over his shoulder, and cups his hands in their direction.

"Forgot to mention…" he yells. "The last name's Grigsby. Horner Grigsby."

FOURTEEN

DISPARU

The window shade is up. Dust particles are playing hide-and-go-seek between intermittent rays of sunshine smiling through the glass. Kyle's world is silent. He twists his head and glares at the hearing aid resting on the nightstand. The molded piece of foreign plastic is his reminder of how thankful he is to hear sound. He inserts the ear piece and flings the comforter off his body, scanning the various, hardly-opened books on the shelf. "*How To Learn French in 30 Days*," he mutters. "Wasn't even close." He sighs. Turning his face to the sunlight, he peers outside, carefully studying the scattered cloud cover. "Strange shapes," he declares, as if waiting for a disembodied voice to agree. The house is quiet. He doesn't hear the customary sound of the weekend vacuum cleaner, or the TV being watched at an annoying volume. "Judy!" he shouts. "Ma! Can you throw in some waffles?" He pauses for the rebuttal, but gets nothing. "Judy! Can you *please* toast some waffles for me?" Waiting for a response, Kyle grabs his leg and scopes out his charred wound. *Hurts even worse today.* He sits up and debates whether to roll out of bed to see what his mom is doing, but succumbs to laziness, falls back into bed, and tries to count the dust particles flying about…"Mom!" he shouts. *Maybe she's in the bathroom taking care of business?* "Gross," he mumbles. Clouds glide across his window frame, like foam on a pond. *Huh…that one kinda looks like a…*he pauses and pivots for the door. "Judy!" he shouts louder, stepping into the hallway. *What's she doing down there?* He pulls the door shut and walks downstairs.

Skyler awakes to the sound of birds chirping outside her partially open window. Her eyes slowly come into focus, zeroing in on the ceiling poster of her idol, Serena Williams. It is the last meaningful gift she remembers getting from her dad before he was sent away. Serena won the French Open that year, and Skyler reminisces how badly she wanted to be just like her, a strong, independent, African-American woman not afraid of any man. "I wonder what he's doing right now?" she says. She rolls on her side and looks out her lone bedroom window, watching the clouds coast by. "You did this to yourself, you know, it was never my fault," she says aloud. With unfocused eyes, she drifts into a trance, staring at all the uniquely distinguishable shapes hidden in the sky. "I wanna' be a cloud…" she mumbles,

"…float away, break apart, and form again, but stronger than Serena…somewhere my dad doesn't exist." Skyler snaps back into focus and glances at the bookshelf. *"How To Learn French in 30 Days,"* she mumbles. "That was a lie," she snips, rolling her eyes. Noticing how eerily quiet it is in the house, she pirouettes to the door and turns the knob. "Hey, Mama! You down there?" she shouts. "Can you cut me up a grapefruit?" Her mom, Cici, is usually quick to fix her up with whatever she needs, but there's no answer. *Maybe she's outside.* Skyler gently shuts the door behind her and walks downstairs.

"Ugh, my room's a wreck!" says Nia, twirling her ponytail. "Nia, Nia, never keeps things clean." She looks at her messy shelf and sees a book from a class she took with her crew. "Ha," she blurts. "No one learns French in 30 days!" She flips out of bed and kicks her "I heart Fox Mulder" tee-shirt across the room, hitting the dresser. Zig-zagging her way through the maze of clothing on the floor, she leans on the windowsill and watches the clouds hovering in the blue sky. "They're like big spaceships…*no*…maybe the rain from the clouds feeds the alien pods that are *already* in the ground. Pod babies." She looks down and sees the smirking Mulder staring back at her from the floor as if he's in agreement. "Yeah, I think so, too, Fox," she says. "But they might be allergic to water…*which* would suck for them." Nia peers out the window again and notices a distinct cloud in the shape of a flower. She watches it shift in size as one of the petals grows and bumps into a larger cloud. "Such a bloom," she says. She turns around to look at the purple iris on her desk. "What do you think, Mommy?" She smiles, glancing back at the flower cloud one last time, disappointed that it's melded with the larger one, creating a sort of jumbled mess, much like her room. She absorbs the silence and wonders why she can't hear the lawnmower outside. Her father always cuts the grass on Saturday morning, even in the rain. She spins to face the open bedroom door and cups her hands to her mouth. "Daddy, hey!" she yells. "Let's go out for breakfast." There's no reply. She walks to the edge of her room where the carpet meets the hardwood of the hallway and cups her hands again. "Papa! You there? Breakfast, *let's go!*" Flustered by the lack of response, she swings the door closed and walks downstairs.

"It's freezing in here," Michael says groggily. The air conditioning fan is blowing on high speed, rattling the window pane. He reaches for a second blanket at the foot of his bed and pulls it over his chest. "I don't smell any food," he says. Tilting his head backward, he aims his voice at the open door. "Mami, the burritos! Fix me up," he shouts, eyeballing the upside-down bookshelf. *French in 30 days? I*

barely know Spanish, and that took twelve years. The noisy rattle of the window draws Michael's attention away from the shelf and toward the sky. He slinks out of bed, and drags his body to the window wrapped in the comforter, like an undead mummy. The clouds roll by like a parade of dream catchers, each woven with a shape more unique than the next. He searches for animal faces, and insects, anything to sidetrack him from thinking about the astral encounter he had with the man in the lab coat. "I gotta tell them about it," he says, fogging the window with his breath. He draws a head with no eyes and no nose, only a slit for a mouth on the window, then wipes it away. "Mom! I'm hungry! You down there?" he shouts. He loosens his grip on the comforter, dropping it to the floor. "Ugh, where is that woman?" he says. Feeling purposely ignored, Michael marches out of his room, slams the door shut, and stomps down the hall.

Kyle, believing Judy is playing possum, tip-toes down each step, trying to get the jump scare on her. He peeks around the corner, but doesn't see her. Instead, he sees the wall phone on the floor, spilled water near a broken glass, a pair of her shoes, and the porch door busted off the hinges. "Judy!" he shouts. There's no response. Kyle grabs the phone and dials out.

"9-1-1, what's your emergency," the woman on the other end of the line replies.

Skyler is halfway down the staircase when she feels an updraft in her face. Thinking she left the foyer door open, she hurries down the remaining steps before stopping in her tracks. There's no door. It's ripped from the frame and lying in the lawn. Her mom's shoes are perfectly positioned at the threshold, and no sign of Mom. "Mama!" she cries out, falling to her knees. Skyler does the only thing she knows to do.

"9-1-1, what's your emergency," the man on the other line replies.

◎

"Dad, hey, yo, Dad, about that breakfast! Forget it, let's just eat here," says Nia, butt-sliding down the carpeted stairwell. Reaching the bottom, she stands up and immediately realizes something is wrong. Her dad's favorite hat, shoes, cell phone, and a long kitchen knife are sprawled out in front of the opened door. "Daddy!" she yells frantically, and remembers what her father taught her.

"9-1-1, what's your emergency," the woman on the other end of the line replies.

◎

Michael storms his way down the hardwood stairs to demand an answer from his mom about breakfast, but trips on the last step. "Gotta be kidding me," he says, dusting himself off. When he lifts his head, he sees the door's missing. His mom's purse, shoes, and car keys are scattered on the floor. The baseball bat they keep in the broom closet is shattered in three pieces across the room, blackened with char marks. "Mami!" he shouts, running to the phone.

"9-1-1, what's your emergency," a raspy voice on the other end of the line replies.

"My mom—gasp—my mom is—"

"…with us, Michael. We have them all."

The phone cuts out.

FIFTEEN

SOUTHERN YELLOW PINE

"Take a picture of the bat," says the detective, pointing to a deputy. "And get the keys and shoes by the threshold! I want everything cataloged and documented. I don't want no foolin' around, ya' hear? Lord knows if I don't keep my thumb on this, you'll screw it all up."

Detective Ray "Spider" Dansby, is Cobb County's no-frills, dragnet-cop, supernova. Back when the nuclear accident occurred, he was one of the first responders on the scene, but he was new, real green then. Now, at the tail-end of his career, he's a savvy veteran, a bombastic fireball. He spins wide, sticky webs, and catches every wrongdoer who flies by.

Dansby, jingling loose change in his pocket, walks into the kitchen where the friends are seated at the table, consoling one another. A pot with steam still rising from earlier that morning intensifies his feeling of empathy for the kids. "Hey, ya'll," he says. "I'm Detective Ray Dansby, but people call me—"

"Spider," answers Kyle, nodding. "Everyone knows who you are."

"Well, I guess my reputation precedes me. Hope it's not a bad thing. Ya'll holding up as best you can?"

Nia buries her head into Kyle's shoulder.

"Look here, we're gonna' put all our resources together to find your parents. I got the entire county and surrounding cou—"

Kyle lifts his head, wiping a tear from his cheek. "With all due respect, sir, your resources won't be able to find them."

"Son, I assure you that whatever it is you think is happening, our resources will track…"

"You saw them then?" quips Skyler. "Your resources been chased before? Were you in danger?" she says, blowing her nose. "Because we just ran through a bunch of old woods by the cemetery, and almost didn't make it out because of those *things*." She looks at Kyle's leg. "Show it to him, Kyle."

"Show me what?" says Dansby.

Kyle sticks his leg out from under the table and reveals his calf.

"That's some kinda…*wound* you got there, young man. Ridin' shotgun on a motorcycle?" he says, forcing a contrite laugh. "Burnt your leg on the exhaust? Naw, I'm just teasin'. You don't have to answer."

"You know who it was. It was *them*. I'd bet you've seen those marks before," says Kyle.

"I've seen…" he stops. "Well, uh, look, your Godparents have been contacted and they'll be here shortly. Ya'll alright here for now? I got to shove off and see about corralling information in the other counties. Deputy Shane Wasser is gonna' hang here till your family arrives. That be okay?"

Kyle retracts his leg and lays his head on the table.

"Alright then," Dansby says, nodding. "Hang tight. We'll get them back. I'm gonna do everything I can to find them. I promise." He taps the wall and walks into the hallway, jingling the change in his pocket.

"I wonder what she was cooking," says Kyle, staring at the stovetop. "She's such a great cook."

"It's just boiled water," replies Michael. "She does it to humidify the room."

"I wish it were breakfast burritos," says Nia, prying her head from Kyle's shoulder. "They're alive, right?"

"There's no doubt," says Skyler. "Our parents are like the most rock-solid, strongest people…But we gotta get back in that attic, Michael. There's gotta be more up there that we didn't find—stuff that Mr. Grigsby talked about. There could be tons of files on this, things people kept secret. Plus, I don't know if I trust Dansby."

"We have a little time until my Uncle gets here," says Michael. "What should we tell Deputy Wasser we're doing?"

"I wouldn't worry about Wasser. He looks like a newbie. I think we can tell him anything, and he'll believe it," says Skyler, smirking.

They get up from the table, and walk into the hallway where Deputy Wasser is taking pictures. Michael turns to look back at the stove and notices the steam has stopped rising. "*We're getting you home, ma'*," he says, standing at the stairway.

"Where *ya'll* going?" asks Wasser.

"Gotta get my stuff for when my Uncle comes. They're just helping me carry it."

"Yeah, oh…*well*, okay."

Newb.

One by one, Michael ushers them up the stairs, into the hallway. "That's weird," he says, looking at the attic door. "It's disconnected from the hinges."

"What happened to your door, dude?" says Nia.

"I have no idea." He gives it a slight shove against the wall, securing it so it doesn't topple over. Kyle slips around him, and as the others climb the stairwell, Michael glances back. "Watch that step," he calls out, reminding them of the brittle 2"x10" plank. *"Don't move,"* he says to the door.

"Mike, get in here, quick!" shouts Kyle.

"What? What is it?"

"Look at that."

"Shadow People? Why would there be a random piece of paper with that on it?"

"You guys think we might have missed that when we got chased outta here by your mom?" asks Nia.

"Maybe. But I didn't see anything fall."

"Noo, but that newspaper article was torn—the one we found. We never could finish the sentence."

"So, *they knew* even back then..."

"See, alwayyyys a conspiracy!" says Nia.

"Makes me wonder what else they knew," says Michael. He flips a lid on one of the file boxes and starts rummaging through it.

"What are we even looking for?" asks Skyler.

"Stuff, just stuff. More clippings. Maybe there's missing person's reports."

"Ya'll good up there!?" shouts Deputy Wasser.

"Yeah! Good! Be down…" yells Michael. "*Newb.*"

"Mike, I have to use the bathroom, is the one downstairs okay?" asks Nia.

"Can't you hold it?"

"Should I go right here?"

"Ugh, Deputy Newb is down there. Use

the one in the bedroom. Sink's broken, though."

Germs. Nia walks down the stairs backward, pausing at each step to make a goofy face at Michael each time he buries his head into the file box. "Sink's broken," she says mockingly.

"Shut up. Hey, I ever tell you about that staircase? It's just regular old wood. Nothing special. But when my dad was stationed in Norfolk, Virginia on a four-year stretch, he and a buddy brought back a big chunk of wood. See, his service time was up, and he wanted a local keepsake. He used that wood to make that—"

"Who cares!" she says, treading backward. *Step...*

Crash.

"It was…southern yellow pine," he says, slapping his forehead. "You cracked his custom step."

"No, sorry, I *destroyed* the step. My foot's stuck."

The others scamper down the stairs to

Nia. Michael lags. The side of her ankle is bleeding, and her shoe is lodged between two splintered pieces of the pine.

"Mike, I'm gonna' have to snap this off."

"But that's—"

"Well, my foot is jammed, so I have to."

"Let me help at least." He pulls on the fractured plank, loosening her foot. Kyle tugs on the other side, freeing her.

"Hey, what's that?" asks Skyler.

Their heads meet in the middle, peering into the hole.

"Cigar box," says Nia.

"What's a cigar box doing *under* the stairs?"

Michael reaches in and pulls it out. "Dusty too," he says, blowing the top, like an old Nintendo cartridge. He carefully lifts the lid and finds a lone, folded newspaper clipping.

"Open it."

Skyler and Kyle's eyes meet. And like a 10,000-watt lightbulb exploding over their heads, they shout, "That's the sister!"

Police fear worst as local woman goes missing

By LAWRENCE SZOLLOSY
DAILY NEWS

Police officers in Pennsylvania have been urged to assist in locating Ruth Ann Grigsby, 42, of White Tanks, Pennsylvania, who has been missing from her home since July. She was seen leaving Derndoff's convenience store around 9:00 p.m. on July 3. The missing woman is described as weighing about 135 pounds and is almost five foot eight inches tall.

Witnesses say Grigsby was seen running from the building, but lost sight of her as she disappeared into the night.

Cody Jones, of Bressler, son of Grigsby, called police after growing concerns that something was wrong after not being able to reach her by phone. Police officers noticed the door to her house was open. A pair of shoes was found at the door, along with a telephone receiver on the floor. There were signs of a struggle. A reward has been offered for information concerning Ruth Ann's whereabouts. She was last seen near Demp Brothers Stone Quarry. Local police should be notified.

THIS WEEKEND

Great Green Tree Festival

"But why's my dad hiding this under his step?"

"*That's* the better question," says Nia.

Michael folds the newspaper and shoves it in his pocket. "I guess there's only one place we gotta go."

"Demp Brothers!" says Nia.

"What about the deputy?" asks Kyle.

There's a short pause.

"Newb!" they shout.

SIXTEEN

SKYLER COOPER

I can never find aces. Skyler places the five of clubs below the six of diamonds, and flips another card from the pile, hoping to find a red four or black seven to add to the tableau. *How can I build properly on just one ace?* The table she's sitting under, cross-legged, has barely enough roof space for the top of her head to fit. *Mom and Dad need a new kitchen table. How's a nine-year-old supposed to play solitaire comfortably?* The cards in her pile are running dangerously low, and she never cheats to win. *You did this to me yesterday.* The three cards left in the stock pile have no rebuttal. Thinking of her next move, she stares out the oxidized, cloudy window above the sink and sees a cardinal pecking at the birdfeeder. *Mom says when a cardinal comes to visit, it's really a loved one who passed on. I wonder who's stopping by today. Maybe it's Grandpa Claude. Grandpa Claude, what would you do if you were in my shoes?* The cardinal erratically lifts its head up from the seed trough, crooks its neck, and peers in at Skyler. It bows its head again, pecking at the seed, then glares into the kitchen. *He wants me to take a card.* She pauses, takes a calculated breath, squints her eyes, and slowly grabs the top card with her index finger and thumb. *An ace!* Skyler snaps her fingers, smiles, and looks to the cardinal, but all she sees is the birdfeeder swaying side to side. *Catch you later, Grandpa.*

At the end of the long hallway leading away from the kitchen, inaudible yelling spills out from the gap in her parents' bedroom door. Skyler leans back and sees shadows pacing back and forth under the threshold. *Another fight.* With a shaky hand, she places the ace on a blank row in the tableau. Looking out the kitchen window, she hopes to spot the cardinal. Nothing. *I'm on my own, again.* A tremendous thud at the end of the hallway is followed by a scream and a crash that sounds like a giant oak tree smashing into a boat dock.

Slam!

"That's the end of it!" yells a male voice. Skyler sees muscular bare legs from the knees down, white socks, and three diagonal stripes on the shoes. Her father's Adidas are marching toward the kitchen. Skyler covers her mouth with her hand to not make a sound, and stares at the ace of hearts, pretending she's one of the playing card characters in *Alice In Wonderland*.

Crash!

Like hail falling in slow motion during a rare February thunderstorm, hundreds of glass shards bounce off the floor and chair, landing in all directions on her solitaire cards.

The piercing noise instinctively shifts her hands from her mouth to her ears. She watches powerlessly as her father stomps his way to the living room, where he sits down and anxiously taps his feet. Skyler looks at the window and can now clearly see the birdfeeder through the forearm-sized hole her father had left. It has stopped swaying. *Mom*, she thinks, waiting for her father's next move.

He stands up and calmly walks toward the living room entrance door that connects to the garage, turns the knob, and closes the door behind him.

Now's my chance. She quietly slithers from the table and sprints down the hallway, opening the bedroom door. The entire bed has been flipped. *"Mom!?"* she shrieks.

"Here, Skyler. I'm here." Her mom's voice is muffled. She's pinned to the floor by the entire frame of the bed.

"I can get you out," Skyler says.

"Baby, no you can't," she gasps. "It's too

heavy. Just call for help."

"*Did Dad—*"

"Call for help."

"*No.*"

Skyler bends at the knees and grips the side rails of the upside-down bed with both hands and stands up with it, gritting her teeth. Her mom crawls away from her entrapment, watching in astonishment as Skyler lifts the bed and flips it right side up with a resounding thud.

"Baby…"

"—gasp, you're safe now, Mama."

"How did you…"

"Call the police."

Realizing something remarkable just happened, Skyler stares at her hands and clenches her fists, knowing she's capable of superhuman strength. She leaves the bedroom and hears the distant rumble of an engine starting. *That's the caravan.* She listens to the slow, squeaky motor of the garage door opening.

He's trying to leave! She dashes into the living room and reaches for the garage doorknob, but it won't turn. "Dad! *Hey*! Open the door! Dad, you can't leave!" she screams. *I won't let you.*

Reversing stride until her back touches the wall, she grits her teeth, squares her shoulders, and sprints full speed with the force of a brahma bull.

Boom!

The door blasts off its hinges and smashes into the driver's side door, where her dad is sitting. "I told you you're not leaving!" she says.

"Skyler, move *out of the way*!" shouts her father. The garage door fully opens and a rush of wind sucks out the choking car exhaust like an Arizona dust devil.

She positions herself in front of the hood with clenched teeth. "I'm *not* moving."

"Skyler…"

"No, Dad."

"Skyler, you're making me…" He revs the car engine.

In the distance, police sirens echo. Neighbors stumble out of their homes, spilling into the street to witness the uproar.

Skyler slams two powerful fists into the hood, denting the frame. She bends her waist in an offensive posture and pushes her body against the car.

"Skyler, if you don't move, I'm gonna have to…"

She feels the horsepower of the van thrust against her arms, but it won't budge. Her hands are vice grips, bending the hood backward, like peeling a sardine can. Swirls of white smoke spew from the spinning back tires and acrid, black smoke rises from under the hood. Skyler's dad has the petal to the floor, but the van won't move. Police cars screech to a halt at the end of the driveway, and officers rush to her aid. The minivan's engine makes a clunking sound and dies. She's crumpled the intake manifold. The garage is enveloped in smoke. "No more," she says, glaring at her dad.

Skyler emerges from the smoke-filled garage, like a ghost in the darkness. Approaching the officers, she points to the garage and says, "He's in there," then falls to the ground.

"*What was that thud?*" yells Deputy Wasser from Michael's kitchen.

"Hey, get up!" says Michael.

"*Is she bleeding?*" asks Nia.

"Get a towel—there's a gash," says Kyle. "And move the door over there."

Michael nods. "I don't know how it fell; I secured it against the wall."

"Yeah, but why is it even off the hinges anyhow?" Kyle asks.

"What's going on up there?" Wasser presses.

"She just tripped," shouts Michael. "We're good."

"I want you kids down here."

"Skyler, you alright?" asks Michael.

"I'm okay," she replies.

"Let's get you up. Deputy *Newb* is getting impatient. That was some shot you took to the head! The door fell on you when you walked out of the attic."

"Door?"

"Yeah," Michael points to the blood stain on the top corner. It almost knocked your eye out!"

"*Now!*" yells Wasser.

They make their way down to the stairway landing.

"What happened to your head?" he asks Skyler, grimacing.

"Nothing. I fell," she says, looking out the kitchen window. A cardinal is perched on the birdfeeder.

SEVENTEEN

DEMP BROTHERS SECRET

"Thank you, officer," says Michael's uncle, walking through the door. "I appreciate you keeping an eye on Michael and his friends during this difficult time."

Wasser answers Michael's uncle's questions to the best of his ability, but is anxious to head out and participate in the search. "Please don't hesitate to call Detective Dansby if you need anything," says Deputy Wasser, tipping his cap as he leaves.

Michael runs to hug his uncle. "You kids

alright?" he says, squeezing Michael's shoulders.

"Uncle Rob, I missed you," Michael says, wiping a tear.

"Hey, mijo, we're blood. Family's family. That goes for you too, kids."

"How was the drive?"

"Long. If you don't mind, I'm going to grab whatever drink your mom keeps in the fridge and lie down for a spell. I hope she has more than just that nasty green health stuff. You guys cool hanging out?"

"Yep, we're good."

"Perfecto."

Kyle shoves Michael in the direction of the door, and snaps his fingers to the others.

"Outside…*now*," he whispers.

"Tell me we're going to the quarry to look for Ruth Ann Grigsby," says Nia. "Do I have time to change? I have this super cool shirt of this—"

"No, Nia, we gotta leave now while there's still light. Mike, tell your Uncle we're going…

to like…we're going to the basketball court or something."

"I don't have a basketball."

"*Mike!*"

"Right. *Uncle Rob! Going to play basketball. We'll be back!*" he shouts, as they scurry down the driveway.

Demp Brothers Stone Quarry has always been considered a place of mystique among kids in White Tanks. Before the fences were built, it was an unofficial hangout where kids ditched school to fish in one of the various natural retention ponds on the property. There were specific nicknames for each locale, like *The Dynamite Shack Pond*, which housed a tiny, red shed, that, at one time, stored dynamite. It has since been emptied and decommissioned. Teenagers started rumors that giant water snakes would drown anyone who swam in it. There was a rogue canoe that drifted aimlessly, and the dare was to see who could swim to it without being taken by the water snakes. *Clay*

Pond, or Tri-color pond, was like something out of an R.L. Stine story. It was horseshoe-shaped, with three waterways intercepting. The far-right side was brackish, stagnant water that had a dilapidated boat dock jutting into it. It smelled of death with the rotting carcasses of sun fish floating on top. The middle section was a bright turquoise that mimicked what water might look like on an alien planet. A small whirlpool in the center sucked everything it touched into a mysterious abyss. The far-left side was clay. Kids would throw rocks to watch them sink slowly. No person ventured close to its edge, for one slip meant certain death. *Top of the World*, which, by stark contrast, wasn't a pond at all, was a heaping pile of shale waste that acted like a small mountain where successful climbers could see for miles, well past Marathon Island. Kids played King of the Hill there, wrestling their way to its apex. Then there was the *Junk Pond*. The Junk Pond was the most difficult pond to reach because of the steady patrol of quarry cops. One of the challenges of even going to Demp Brothers was dodging the security that roamed the grounds. Trees acted as cover from the power-hungry, overzealous, fake-mall cops who had nothing better to do than bust adventurous kids. Deerberry bushes became camouflage triages to treat thorny plant injuries. The old quarry was a whole other world before it had become Ft. Knox, with its ironclad fence system.

"We have about an hour before dark," says Kyle. "I don't need another cemetery encounter."

"Really? Why? Maybe I do. Maybe we'll find our parents in the dark," barks Skyler.

"No, we'll be dead."

"You don't know that."

"Yes, he does," says Michael. He lifts his head from kicking rocks and can see the shale chute at Demp Brothers in the distance. "I have to confess. The night in the woods…No, forget it, you'll think I'm nuts."

"Go ahead, Mike," says Skyler, sensing embarrassment.

"The night in the cemetery woods when I blacked out. I didn't *really* blackout. I projected. Astral projection. Ever hear of it?"

"Wasn't that an Atari game?" asks Nia.

"No, space cadet. Astral Projection. I can travel dimensions, my body...well, my *astral body*. Remember how I got weirded out at Mr. Grigsby's place? Everyone shook his hand but me. He talked about his brother Martin, the scientist dude at Marathon Island—the guy responsible..."

"Yeah."

"I met him."

"*You what?*"

"He...*he* had a lab coat, and a hard hat; he looked old and craggy. He was holding a clipboard with a diagram of the nuclear plant blowing up. His arms were blackened...like burnt, and then he faded into the cemetery toward two steam towers mumbling inaudible things. He warned me to get you guys out of those woods, like he *knew* about the shadowpeople. He was all charred. I…"

"*I believe you*," says Nia.

"You do?"

"I have a confession too. I developed a mutation in my eyes when I was five."

"Shut. Up!" says Kyle, sarcastically.

"No for real," she says. "It's called Scotopsin. I can see in the dark, and I can see ultraviolet light, like animals do."

Michael throws his hat to the ground. "Ah, ha! That's why you kept saying *I am the light*!"

"When my mom died, she told me to be *the light*, to light the path."

Kyle stops just short of the quarry fencing and turns around. "I have sonic hearing."

Michael falls to the ground laughing, like he's been pumped with nitrous oxide. *Sonic hearing*!

"Prove it!"

"Fine. Go over there, like, way over there. Take Skyler. Whisper something to her."

Michael grabs Skyler's hand and they run far from earshot. Michael leans in to Skyler but before he can pull his head away, Kyle smiles.

"You said you think Nia has a weird crush on Fox Mulder."

"What!?" shouts Nia. "Mike!"

"This is *cra-zee*," says Michael. "All this time. Wait, let me guess. Hold up…hold up. Skyler, *you* can fly!"

"Nope," she says.

"Naw, go ahead. Flap your arms. Let's see it," he says, motioning his arms.

"Hey, how are we getting into the quarry?" asks Nia.

"We'll just break through the fence," says Skyler.

"It's fortified steel with razor wire!"

"And?"

"Oh no…"

Skyler spreads her hands like eagle talons

and grips the fencing, looking around to see if anyone else is watching them.

"...*heh*...break the fence..." Michael says, snickering. "Yeah..."

Skyler grits her teeth and starts prying the fencing apart with her hands until the metal twists and screeches. Snapping the steel braids with a pop, she slowly stretches a body-sized bore hole. "*See*...break the fence," she says, closing Michael's gaping mouth. "I have superhuman strength. I just chose not to freak ya'll out. I had it since I was nine. I just didn't want to feel like a freak."

"None of us did," says Michael.

"I guess we're all freaks," says Nia.

Skyler steps away from the fence and looks at her friends. "So, who's going through first?"

EIGHTEEN

THEY BECOME YOU

The low summer sun is falling, scattering its light between the pines like sparkling pixie dust. The temperature is dropping. "We have about an hour," Kyle says, glancing at his phone.

"Less," says Skyler, looking at hers.

"Which way to the Junk Pond?" Nia asks.

Everyone turns and looks at Michael.

"What?" he says, lifting his head. "Hey, I haven't been everywhere in my astral travels," he says defensively. "It doesn't *always* work." Michael mockingly shoves Kyle in the back, then runs behind a large tree. "Quarry cops—take cover!" The others scurry behind Michael, shading themselves from two passing security guards walking past the Clay Pond. "Hey, *I know*," he whispers sarcastically to Kyle. "Instead of *me*, why don't *you* use your supersonic hearing, or whatever it is you have, and see if you can pick up any trace of her."

"If she's even here."

"Yeah, if she's even here."

"I heard the Junk Pond is abandoned and hidden in some ravine, placed there by ancient aliens that mined—"

"*Nia*," says Michael.

"I'm just saying…"

Kyle closes his eyes and holds his hearing aid firmly, panning the rocky landscape, like a bat echolocating its next meal.

Nia holds her breath.

"…well, he ain't gonna find your aliens," Michael says.

"You never know!"

"*Shhhh,*" says Skyler.

"There." Kyle points. I hear something. *Faintly.* It's a woman's voice, I think. I don't know. It's coming from down there, though."

"What about those guards?" asks Nia.

"Skyler can just…beat them up," Michael says laughing. "You're super girl."

"How 'bout I beat you up instead."

"Guys, c'mon. Daylight's wasting," says Kyle sternly. "We need to make our way down those rocks. I'll harness whatever sound she makes, *you know*, the closer we get to the pond."

"We have to make a run as soon as those quarry cops pass by. Don't fall down," says Skyler. "I'm not turning back for you."

"*Now?*" asks Nia.

"No, wait…"

"Wait…"

"Wait…"

"*NOW!*" They run in the open field, across the dump truck path, zeroing in on a nearby Deerberry bush for cover. "That's the—gasp—path," says Skyler, peering over the edge. "That pond's filthy."

"That's why they call it the Junk—"

"Don't be that guy." She scowls.

They descend the patchwork path, which looks visibly unused for many years. The seldom seen Junk Pond reveals its shapeshifting aquatic cesspit through gaps in the overgrown shrubs and radiated trees. The water is lime green and littered with broken chairs, toilet seat covers, rubber tires, and a half-sunken row boat, which at some point, served the town's bustling life as a fishing vessel—long before the nuclear accident had occurred.

"It looks like time stood still," says Nia.

"Not time," says Kyle. "Radiation."

Kyle stops them. "Look over there," he says, pointing. "I can hear her so clearly now." Tufts of steam rise from a ramshackle hovel, which is burrowed into a shrub-covered cliff of the quarry, purposely veiled from any human activity.

Careful not to snap branches, they slither like snakes across patches of soft crab grass, toward the hut.

"You're walking too heavy, ease up—"

"*Shh*, no I'm not, I'm—"

"*Who's out there?*" snarls a woman's voice, weathered and raspy. They duck behind a bush. "*How many of you's? Go away.*" A rectangular panel in the warped door folds down, and a pair of wrinkled eyes stare out. "*I said away with you.*"

Kyle clears his throat, perched in the bush. "Are you Ruth Ann Grigsby?"

The notch slams shut. "*She's dead,*" the voice says. "*Now go away.*"

"Ma'am, we're, *uhh*, we think we met your brother, Horner..." Kyle unfolds the newspaper clipping of the missing woman and raises it above the bush. "...and we think this is you."

After a long pause, the panel flips back

down and a set of blood-shot eyes squints at the paper.

"They actually looked for me," she snickers. "And we also want to know…" Skyler says, peeking her head above the bush, "…if you were the one who left those cryptic notes on the trees."

"My paper trail," she scoffs. There's a clicking sound, like a bolt slipping through a latch. The door cracks open, revealing the glow of a small fire.

"Should we go in?" whispers Michael. "I feel like it's an invitation."

"Invitation? I don't know…what if she wants to kill us?" says Nia.

"She could be one of the shad…"

"I'm *not the one* who wants to kill you," says the woman.

Kyle gently nudges open the creaky door. They bow their heads below the frame, ducking through. A rusted kettle of water is boiling over an open flame. An elderly woman is sitting on a crooked rocking chair with a scarf tied around her face. Mismatched clothing covers her body like a dyslexic quilt.

"Is that water from the pond?" asks Nia. "Because it's green, and I don't think it's—"

"Lady has to drink," she mutters. "Though, not much longer, I presume." She points a bony, veiny finger at Kyle. "You. Touched your leg, did they? I can smell the ash," she says, closing her eyes, inhaling.

"Why'd you leave those notes?" asks Kyle.

The woman ignores his inquiry. "*And you…*" She points to Michael, "…I've seen *you*. The night I was taken, that was *you* hovering above the house…*watching me…watching* the life I knew be snuffed out, *you*, floating around in my trees. You haven't aged. *Why*?" she asks.

Michael looks away from her.

Kyle unfolds one of the tree notes, ignoring her incessant interrogation of Michael. "So, you're R.A.G.?" he says, deflecting. "This *is* you."

She rocks in her chair, nods, and pours the hot water into a chipped ceramic mug.

"But why?" asks Kyle.

She sets the mug on a small table, then carefully unwraps her scarf. "*This* is why," she says, uncovering a charred, ashen face. "They came for me. They'll come for you too. The entire town is cursed. Cursed because of me, and because of—"

"*Martin*," interrupts Michael.

"Good *boyyyy*," she hisses, eyes widening. She unwraps the makeshift sleeves she's sewn together, exposing her blackened, charred arms. "*They become you*," she hisses. "They invade your body and feed on your soul like deathly parasites, transforming the human you into a shadowy scourge, birthing an evil in the shape of a darkness only night stalkers can see. They gorge on the wrongdoing bestowed on them— pirating a cruel siege, overtaking the town to brand it their own—to make White Tanks the sort of place it was never supposed to be." She

165

sips from the mug. "This is my cocoon," she says, raising her arms outwardly. "And I will metamorphose…to my demise."

"The wrong done to who?" asks Kyle.

"Those who died that day." She chuckles, remembering the flames. "You can't stop what's coming, my dear." She sighs, then re-wraps the scarf around her face, exposing only her eyes, tipping her head to the decay of the outside light. "Dusk falls, you haven't much time."

"Tell us where our parents are! Tell us where Martin is! Kyle demands. What's happened to them?"

"Fly, fly, fly…," she answers softly. "*Fly, fly, fly, little moths.*" She rotates her chair away from them to face the crackling fire. *When black breeze blows through, is when they become you.* Her voice lowers to an inaudible murmur. *When black breeze blows through, is when they become you.* Kyle stares at the note.

"C'mon, man, we gotta go," says Michael to Kyle. "I don't like any of this."

Nia looks out the door and no longer sees the waning sun. "Kyle, we have to go, *now!*"

"No, wait…"

When black breeze blows through, is when they become you, she whispers, whistling.

Skyler tugs on Kyle's shirt, pulling him out the door. Through the small rectangular panel, he sees Ruth Ann's shadow flickering erratically against the wall, as she repeats the same phrase in his inner ear.

When black breeze blows through, is when they become you. She giggles.

As they jog to the entrance of the ascending path, Kyle winces, sensing a human frequency trespassing in his ear. He stops, closes his eyes, and grabs for the hearing aid, eavesdropping on the muffled message transmitting through.

"Heed the echo. Duggan Brothers—that is where you'll find *it.* And all go goodnight into that malicious abyss," she taunts.

Midway up the path, they stop to peer into the gorge, taking notice that the once billowy steam that arose upon their arrival has been extinguished.

It was the last they saw of Ruth Ann Grigsby.

NINETEEN

TILLING THE WEEDS

"Found this guy pickin' dandelions in your front yard, Michael," Detective Dansby says as he walks into Michael's house.

Deputy Wasser scowls, unamused.

"Awe, c'mon, *Wasser*, lighten up. I'm just foolin' about," he says, playfully slapping his cheek. "How you kids doin'? Ya'll alright?" he asks, inspecting the house. "Got me a couple leads from anonymous tips," he says, staring at Kyle. "Some folks been sayin' they seen a few of your parents."

Kyle rolls his eyes.

"Yeah, I know, boy. You ain't got faith in the system." He chuckles. "Ol' Dansby knows how this thing works—don't you worry 'bout that," he says, opening the refrigerator.

Skyler sees Kyle clench his fist, and knows he wants to punch Dansby. She shakes her head at Kyle not to.

"You don't mind if I…" Dansby scours the shelf looking for something to drink. "… grab me a cool one. Say, what's this here green stuff?"

"That's my mom's…"

"Yeah, uhh, nevermind that drink. Say, uhh, so here's the deal…" Dansby closes the fridge door and notices Kyle's leg. "Got yourself a little limp there, ay, boy? That wound got bigger I reckon. Matter fact, looks way bigger, blacker than moonshine at midnight, too."

"Not really. I hardly feel it," replies Kyle.

"Bullswap. Don't look like no motorcycle

burn now does it? You ain't got nothin' to say about it?"

"Like I said…I hardly feel it."

"*Uh huh*…I see. Well, Wasser n' me gonna hightail it outta here then. Just wanted to shine a little news. I gotta drop Wasser off at bingo. It's basket night. Ain't that right, deputy?" he says, smacking his cheek.

"I hate that guy," whispers Kyle.

"Imagine how Wasser feels," quips Nia.

Skyler peeks her head around the living room archway at Michael's Uncle who is watching TV. "You find a basketball yet, Mike?" she asks.

"A basketball? Why?"

"Cause you keep telling your Uncle we're going to play basketball, and we never have a basketball! Looks suspect!"

"Yeah, but why are we playing basketball?"

"We're not," Kyle says. "We're going to Fort Bliss." He leaves without waiting for the others to follow. "I have a basketball."

"Should we go with him…But my uncle… *Kyle wait*," Michael shouts. "Uncle Rob, we're gonna go play bask—"

"Yeah, go, go. Be back by dark!"

Skyler, Nia and Michael catch up to Kyle who's rounding the corner to his house. "*Hey*, slow down!" says Skyler, pulling on Kyle's shoulder.

"No," he says, pointing to his hearing aid. "I heard her."

"Who?"

"The old lady."

"When?"

"Back at the quarry, climbing up the path."

"What'd she say?"

"Said we'd find *it* at Duggan Brothers."

"Who it?"

"Shadowpeople," says Michael.

"Something about hearing an echo and she rambled about a malicious abyss," says Kyle. "I think she was dying, rambling things. It doesn't make sense. This is why we gotta put our heads together at Bliss, and figure this out. I want our parents back."

"Word," says Nia. "I miss my daddy."

They walk by Mrs. Peterson's run-down house, old Roy and his barking cocker spaniel that patrols the fence, Mary Winchester's duplex with the broken shutters, and Mr. Landis who has a shabby green couch for a porch bench.

"Where do you think they are?" asks Nia.

"The shadowpeople?" replies Kyle.

"No, our parents."

"Hopefully safe."

"Know what I think?" says Michael. "I think the whole town's turning. All of 'em."

"No chance," says Kyle.

"Yeah? So, you *haven't* been noticing how everyone wears long pants and shirts around here? It's crazy hot out. You're tellin' me they might not be hiding something—something like what's on your leg."

"I mean…"

"What's the last thing you remember your

mom wearing?"

"I didn't notice, I guess. I dunno, jeans and a henley, maybe?"

"Yeah, covered up."

"Look, *I'm the one* with the conspiracy theories around here, not you guys!" shouts Nia. "Stop it. We're going in."

Entering the woods from Cedar Street, they notice from a distance Horner Grigsby tending to his vegetable garden through a gap in the maple trees.

Michael sighs in relief. "No bullets today," he says.

As if he'd heard him, Horner stops pruning weeds, stands up, turns around, stares straight in their direction, cracks a dry smile, then postures like he's holding a fake rifle, takes aim at them, and pulls the trigger. Lowering his imaginary weapon, he laughs and salutes them.

"No, Mike…not anymore," says Kyle, tipping his cap to Horner.

"Kyle, you sure your leg's alright?" asks Michael. "Dansby was right. It *is* bigger. You're limping too. You're trying to hide it."

"I'm with Mike," says Skyler. "I think it got bigger since we left the house."

"*I'm serious.* I feel fine," replies Kyle. "Maybe it's bigger I guess."

"It's covering most of his calf," whispers Michael to Skyler. "What if it gets worse and he turns into…"

"*No.* Not him," she whispers back. They walk past the faceless man—a nickname given to a boulder shaped like a human head. It's the last familiar landmark before entering the clearing for the giant oak, where the hose ladder is tied.

"Hey, you think anyone else has a hose ladder, like us?" asks Nia.

"No. But then again, they ain't The Flying Tigers either," says Skyler, high-fiving Nia.

"It doesn't look right," says Michael, peering ahead. "Where's the rest of it? Hose looks cut."

"Hey, *shh*, *shh*. Stop!" shouts Kyle. "Get low. I see 'em." Near the big oak, scattered like autumn leaves, are black dolls, like the ones at the Black Path. They're in seated positions, with gaping mouths and jagged, chalk-white teeth.

"They're mocking us," whispers Michael.

Skyler looks at Michael, then rises from her crouch and runs at the dolls, angrily kicking several over the edge of the hill. She fiendishly laughs, and watches them plummet to the rocks below. She picks up another and digs her nails in, piercing its plush body, ripping its limbs apart. "*Not. Any. More.*" She decapitates another, and yanks the cotton stuffing from its neck, launching it into the woods.

"Sky-ler!" yells Kyle, running toward her.

"Not any—gasp—*more*."

"They cauterized the hose," says Nia, holding the charred end of what's left.

"We're gonna have to climb down with what we have," says Kyle. "Mike, maybe you can rig something."

"I'll try," he says. "But I need more cordage."

"Mike, maybe you can rig something. *R-r-*rig something," Kyle stutters.

"Bro, I heard you the first time."

"Maybe you can rig something…*some-thiiiiiing.*"

"What's he doing!?" shouts Nia.

"…rig… something," Kyle says, in a low, guttural voice.

"No!"

His head shakes vigorously from side to side, oscillating like a top. His pupils roll back. Thin, red blood vessels bloom, like tiny tree branches on the whites of his eyes. His body convulses. The wound on his leg flares red, shedding the ashen skin, like water shaken from a wet dog. He collapses. He's breathing, but unconscious.

The others surround him and stare helplessly at his exaggerated chest contractions.

"His eyes are fluttering!" shouts Nia.

"Give him some space, back up a little," says Skyler.

Kyle's eyes snap open as if a shot of pure adrenaline pierced his heart. He appears normal. "What are you guys staring at?"

TWENTY

BREACH

"You're not gonna talk about it?" asks Skyler.

Kyle's limp is noticeably more staggered. He struggles to slog through the snapping branches toward Bliss.

"Wish I could," he replies, turning to look at what was left of the hose ladder in the distance. "But I don't remember."

The silence is deafening.

Nia's eyes widen, staring straight through Michael, telepathically nudging him to speak.

"That was gnarly what you did back there, Kyle, you were like…" Michael rolls his eyes back, "…and then you—"

"What Michael is *trying* to say," Nia cuts in, "is you're getting worse, Kyle. You can barely walk!"

"That's not true…*see*," he says, agitated. Kyle straightens his leg to walk unhindered. "We just need to get to the fort, regroup, and figure this whole thing out." His leg doesn't cooperate the way he wants it to, and the pain forces him back into a limp. "We agree the past few days have been absolutely nuts?"

"Your head spun."

"Like I said…*nuts*."

"Look, I'll just say it," blurts Skyler, yelling back at Kyle. "I think you're turning."

"Turning!" Kyle yells, then snickers.

"And I don't know how much time you have until you're one of *them*," she shouts. "Have you actually looked at your leg, Kyle? That black stuff is growing."

Kyle pushes playfully on Skyler's forehead with his finger. "I'm gonna be alright. I promise," he says.

The creek bridge is just ahead, and Michael notices the landscape is different. It's the middle of summer and leaves on the maple trees have turned brown, some shriveled, like overcooked bacon. Tree bark is charred, fossilized with ghostly handprints of unhuman skin. The air is dense, saturated in a pale smell of rotten meat, with no visible signs of dead animals nearby. The creek is murky, swollen over its bladder. "Tide's coming in," says Michael, staring at its engorged banks. "Rained a ton last night. The thunder woke me up. Ya'll too?"

"Not really," says Nia.

"I kept seeing shadowy shapes in my window when the lightning cracked."

"Maybe it wasn't the lightning."

"Maybe it was them?"

Skyler pauses just short of the flooded bridge, signaling an *all-stop* with her hand.

The others freeze in their tracks, and gawk at what's drifting downstream. A black doll glides above the creek's rolling waves and dips into a rippled current, zipping past Skyler's foot. Another is floating face-up, with a chalk outline smile. Several more erratically seesaw in the water like fishing bobbers. Behind them, like a macabre watery grave, float hundreds of black cotton carcasses, some shredded, with stuffing bleeding out, some wholly intact, each more shudder-inducing than the next.

Dolls, she mutters, kicking one off her shoe.

"They're getting closer…" says Nia, watching them wash by, "…taunting us."

Michael snaps off a stick and measures the depth of the water. Satisfied, he treads across the gully, gingerly pushing his way through the bottleneck of floating phantoms. As he lifts his foot onto drier land, he hears a sucking sound in the rushing water, like a whirlpool in a bathtub drain. *Stupid mud.* His submerged shoe pops off into the waiting arm of a smiling doll that sails by. He yanks out his naked foot from the mud and helplessly watches the gyre sweep his shoe away. *They even took my shoe.* The others, content with Michael's safe passage, tramp through the same wet path and stand by his side. Wearing one shoe—hands in his pockets—Michael frowns at the ruined remains of the structure ahead.

"They got that, too," he mutters, throwing a rock in frustration at the busted door.

"Look at our fort!" shouts Nia.

"*And that,*" says Kyle, pointing.

"That's a stone from the cemetery," says Skyler. She walks over and looks down at the nameplate. Her mom's name is etched on it. Three more stones are arranged in a vertical line leading up to the vandalized fort.

"How can they move those stones?"

"They didn't. They're new, and they have our parents' names on them," says Skyler.

"They're sending a message," says Kyle.

"But soon, we're going to send one back."

Approaching the fort, they see that all the camouflage evergreen branches nailed to the siding have been torn off and shredded; needles cover the ground like AstroTurf. The entrance door is ripped from its top hinge and splintered. Planks of side panel wood are missing and snapped in half. A powdery, black substance blankets the fort, as if it had been scorched by flames.

"Nothing smells burnt," says Kyle.

"No, it smells like death," says Michael.

"I'm going inside." Skyler uses her strength to pry the door from the bent, bottom hinge bolt, tossing it into the shrubs like a toy. The void reveals the vandalized corridor to Ft. Bliss. Their tree stump chairs are covered in ash. Molasses-like slime is slinking down the walls, pooling on the dirt floor, like a vat of toxic sludge.

"Have a look at that," Nia says, tilting her head to the skylight. A ghastly, malnourished face, with sunken, eyeless sockets, and a gaped mouth filled with jagged, rotten teeth is etched into the glass, like holographic carnival art inside a haunted house.

"That's what we become," whispers Skyler, behind Nia. "That's what they want to turn us into."

"The wall!" shouts Kyle, pointing to the back corner. Like splattered, smashed tomatoes, sloppily written words are scratched in black slime and ash on the wall.

RED BENCH

"That's where they are," says Michael.

"The *shadowpeople?*" asks Nia.

"Our parents."

"Where's there?"

Skyler blows the ash off her tree stump seat and sits down. "The one and only place Michael saw a red bench."

"Marathon Island," he whispers.

"That's a suicide mission," says Nia.

"Maybe. But it might be the only way to get them back."

Kyle sits on his tree stump and folds his hands. "There's a guaranteed way to know," he says, looking to Michael.

"*Shadowpeople*," says Michael, sitting down.

"That's where Ruth Ann said I'd find *it*. What else could it be? I say we circle back home." Kyle is hit with a rush of newfound adrenaline. "We'll figure out what to do with Mike's uncle, and we march on Duggan Brothers, *Flying Tigers* style!"

"At night?" asks Nia.

"*You're the light!*" shouts Michael. "Do it for Mommy, right?"

"That's right," says Kyle. "We've all been gifted with something powerful, beyond the normal. We're the abnormal. It's time we use it…*together*…before it might be too late for me," he acknowledges.

Kyle holds his hand out in the middle of their circle and waits for others to pile on.

One by one they lay their hands on Kyle's, posturing for a cheer. Kyle winks at them and orchestrates the rally.

"For Judy."

"For Cici."

"For Jin."

"For Rosa."

"On three…"

"1-2-3…Flying Tigers!"

TWENTY-ONE

LIGHTS OUT

Don't be afraid. A yellow street lamp with a cracked outer casing flickers, enlarging the size of the dangling spiders, making them appear as prehistoric beasts. *It's just a shadow.* With a slight shove, the entrance fence squeaks open. *Go slow, they won't bother you.* Like eight-legged wardens at the entrance to an empty prison, the spiders stop spinning their meal traps and focus their eyes on the frightened trespasser. *Paid the toll.* Steam from the night's rain rises from the crumbling ground, camouflaging the decayed building's facade. *What's happening to me?* Puddles in the concave asphalt act as funhouse mirrors, distorting a face that is human into a ghastly disfigurement. *Stay on.* The flashlight is violently shaken, furiously attempting to resuscitate the dimmed beam shining on the graffitied warehouse walls. *They become you* is written in blood on the peeled green paint. It's a warning. The unlatched door swings open crookedly, bumping a rusted, drum barrel. *Abandoned.* Water droplets from the leaky roof pitter patter onto the puddles covering the floor. *It's freezing in here.* Metal ventilation shutters flap against the stiff wind. Vicious thrashing of the vent panels masks an unidentifiable noise whispering within the darkness. The flashlight falls, bouncing off the floor. *Who's there?* The dancing light illuminates a slender figure that exhibits no discernable human features. It's standing beneath a cracked archway across the warehouse. The wind suddenly stops howling. *Who are you?*

Silence.

Opening its cavernous mouth, it blasts a deafening vocal boom that reverberates the rain puddles, and shakes the room. *No, don't go out!* The flashlight burns dead. Slow, methodical footsteps slosh over the wet floor, growing closer with each echoed splash. *No! Whatever you are, stay away!* With a shake, the flashlight briefly ignites. A black, ashen silhouette erupts from the dirt, dragging him into the earth.

The moon is full. Kyle hovers over Michael's limp body. "Mike, get up, *hey*," Kyle says, shaking him. "You're filthy."

"Is he dead?!" asks Skyler.

"*No*," says Michael, awakening, spitting dandelions from his mouth. "Why's it so dark?"

"All the street lights are out. All the porch lights too. My flashlight won't work either."

"Storm?"

"*You know the reason.*"

Nia turns the corner to Michael's house, sees him sprawled in the grass, and runs to him. "*Whoa*! You're all dirty!"

"Established that," he says.

"You projected?" asks Kyle.

"Reconnaissance mission."

Skyler hands Michael her bottle of water. "Thirsty, huh?"

"I get cotton mouth when I travel."

Kyle kneels beside Michael. "So anyway…"

"There's something at Duggan Brothers," says Michael. He gives the empty bottle back to Skyler. "Pretty sure it's *them*." They help lift Michael to his feet and shake the loose grass and dirt from his clothes. "They're more powerful than I thought."

"We're marching on Duggan Brothers," says Kyle. He nods to the house. "Your uncle's asleep. I heard him snoring in the basement."

"Well then light us up, Nia," says Skyler, looking at the dark telephone poles.

Nia closes her eyes and inhales deeply. Her eyes open, the color of iris purple.

"That's so cool!"

"Mike, can you walk?" asks Kyle.

"My strength'll come. Let's go."

Porch lights are off. Neighbors' dogs aren't barking, owls aren't hooting, even crickets have lost their voice. White Tanks is silent. Cool winds sway power lines between telephone poles, like toy boats rocking in a moonless ocean. The only shining lights are Nia's ultraviolet eyes, reflecting off the pavement.

"Where *is* everybody?" asks Skyler, scanning the streets for any sign of a neighbor or animal.

"I don't like this," says Kyle. "I hear whispers, but nothing I can decipher."

"From which direction?" asks Michael.

"*Everywhere.*"

Michael sees the lone lamp post at the fence entrance to Duggan Brothers Steel Mill. The light within its fractured yellow casing is burned out.

"That's where we go in."

Ten paces away, he diverts his attention to the hole in the plastic casing of the lamp where no spiders are dangling. *No toll tonight.*

Nia presses her nose to the fence. "You went in *there?*"

The gate is locked. "Skyler, can you…"

Bang! She pounds on the slide bolt like an anvil hammering down on a chunk of molten steel, ejecting the lock housing.

Michael swings open the gate and stares into a swollen puddle, observing his non-rippled reflection. *I'm not a monster.*

"Is that the entrance door, Mike?" asks Nia, illuminating peeled green paint, and rust covered lag bolts. Mike nods.

All Go Goodnight into That Malicious Abyss.

"Did you write that to goof on us when you did your astral projection?" asks Kyle, reading the charred words above the door knob.

"Skyler…," says Mike.

Smash! Skyler blasts through the metal door with an overhand right hook, crumpling the bolt casing, splitting the ashen words apart.

"No. It said something different."

Michael presses his thumb to the door, creaking it open. Nia brightens the room. Dead carcasses of large rats lead a bloody trail to an archway across the hollow room.

"That's where it stood," says Michael, wiping a fallen water droplet from his forehead.

"*It?*" asks Skyler.

"*It*—I don't know. It looked like a man, I guess, but it was so pitch dark in here."

"*Shadowpeople…*"

"No, I don't think so, Sky."

Kyle points Nia's head at the archway. "*Shine that way.*"

"Did you go through there?" Nia asks. Her UV light reaches the arch, but doesn't extend into the black oblivion beyond.

"I got pulled into the ground—then you

found me in my yard…so, no."

"Those rats lead back there," says Skyler, nudging one with her boot. "They're eating rats now?" They form hands and walk slowly toward the disintegrating archway. Drips from the leaky roof are the only sound that resonates off the walls.

"My eyes hurt, Mike," says Nia.

Don't go out.

Nia's ultraviolet light flickers, dimming the closer they move to the archway.

"What's wrong with you?" asks Michael. "It really hurts," she says, rubbing her eyes. Her light cuts through the darkness with the decreased power of a worn-out glow stick.

"I'm losing my…"

"*Hold tighter!*" says Kyle. "We have to know what's back there. *Flying Tigers don't let go!*"

They cross the threshold of the arch and enter a domed, mausoleum-like room, dank and smelling of rotten meat. Kyle drops to one knee and grabs at his hearing aid. *Heed the echo,* he remembers. With each wary step forward, a squishing sound bubbles from their shoes.

"I hope that's not blood," says Skyler.

"How far back does this room go?" asks Nia, squinting in distress. Her light is all but drained.

Michael shakes his head. *Don't go out.*

"I can hear them breathing," whispers Kyle, clutching his ears.

"Hear *them*?" panics Michael, tapping on Nia's head for an on-switch.

Hidden in the confines of the corner, behind a rock wall, a piteous voice echoes out.

"*Won't find them,*" it says.

TWENTY-TWO

SKELETON KEY

Dim, purple light shines from Nia's incandescent eyes, unveiling a tapestry of words and phrases etched on the disintegrating walls of the mausoleum.

BLACK BREEZE

CAN'T CHANGE

MAINTENANCE ROOM

FLY, FLY, FLY

TOWERS

MALICIOUS ABYSS

skin WASTE AWAY

END SHALL COME

A thin, haggard old man, shrouded in tattered cloth is slouched against a wall beside a crudely built wooden bed and a pile of crumpled clothes. His hands are sheathed and folded, his face partially concealed by a dingy bandana stained with dried blood.

"I'm delighted you made it, Michael," he says, lazily coughing a laugh. "Is it that time, I suppose?"

"*How did you know his—*"

"I travel, too, Nia. We've crossed astral paths, haven't we, Michael?"

The man points at Kyle. "And you, with the wizard ears. You hear *them*...don't you? They seethe inside your brain, like nightcrawlers squirming through the wet dirt."

"I..."

"*Yessss,*" he hisses. "I know it to be true."

The man shifts his aching legs, grunts in discomfort, and unwraps the garment from around his face, revealing a bony-cheeked, recessed face, littered with large, black lesions.

Half his jaw has eroded, exposing elongated gums and teeth.

"My face frightens you?"

"It…"

"*They become you.*"

Michael glances at the mound of clothing next to the bed, noticing a partially folded white lab coat.

"You know *who* I am, Michael. You don't need the coat for confirmation." He looks at Skyler. "I sense you want to say something, strong girl. Proceed with what you know is true."

"*Martin,*" announces Skyler.

The facial contortion of his wry smile detaches a cracked piece of his ashen face.

"*Eww,*" blurts Nia and Skyler.

He looks down at the floor. "Apologies for that. Won't be missing it."

"Mind if I stand up?" he asks. "I thought it courteous to ask first. My body can be quite intimidating upon initial encounter."

"It's your...*house*," says Skyler, scanning the room.

Martin unhinges his creaky knees, and presses his back against the wall, slithering into a crooked stance.

"*Yesss*," he breathes. "Much better."

He tilts his head back, closes his eyes, and inhales deeply through flared nostrils, then looks at Kyle. "They touched yo*u*," he says, pointing to his leg.

The foul-smelling, towering man limps over to Kyle, reeking of rancid meat. "In time, you, too, shall run out of..."

"Enough with the riddles, Martin, tell us where our parents are!" Michael demands.

"*Tsk, tsk, tsk*, Michael." Martin slides his feet closer to the edge of the room. "I enjoy your enthusiastic...*charm*." He admires the graffitied wall, staring at several words above the archway. His eyes widen. "But the poorly timed execution is, how do you say...*rude*. And I don't particularly enjoy insolent people,

Michael."

Piece by shredded piece, Martin removes section of his frayed sleeves, unveiling more ashen abrasions on what's left of his human forearms. He picks up a piece of white chalk from the floor and begins drawing in a void on the wall. As he presses on the chalk, a fingernail breaks off and falls to the ground. "Forgive me," he says. "Transformation."

The chalk skips across the uneven surface of the decaying concrete wall, swirling and looping, sweeping up and down, and left to right. His scrawny hand dances with the chalk, like a morbid maestro conducting a ghoulish symphony. His eyes are closed and his body is swaying side to side, drifting blindly to the tune of silent melody.

"You're listening to classical music," says Kyle. "It's Mozart."

Martin stops drawing and turns to Kyle. "*Lacrimosa.* Verrrry good," he says, continuing to draw.

"Wait, you can hear music *in his ears?*" asks Nia.

"*I*…this is the first time I ever…" Kyle closes his eyes to think. "It means *weeping* in Latin," answers Kyle, confused.

Martin again turns to Kyle and smiles. "Right again." He momentarily stops sketching, and stares blankly at the wall. "I allowed the feed pump to malfunction. The turbine water could not remove the heat from the steam generator. The fuel pellets melted." He continues drawing. "Boom."

"Yeah, but, okay, you were in charge," says Nia. "Accidents happen. Why all the hiding and drama?"

He stops drawing again and frowns. "Wasn't an accident. My sister and I were going to be terminated. We made other, more, unabashed plans."

"You did it *on purpose!?*"

The remaining nub of the chalk snaps and crumbles to the wet floor. Martin rubs his hands free of the dust and steps away from the wall.

Kyle can no longer hear the music in Martin's ears.

Martin reveals a scaled model of Marathon Island, complete with the two remaining steam towers, the rocky shoreline, barbed wire fencing, a room marked "Maintenance," and an "X" where they should enter. It's an exact replica of what Michael saw on the clipboard in the cemetery.

"This was your fault all along," says Kyle. "You *killed* those people."

"Everything ends where it begins, and begins where it ends," replies Martin.

Skyler points to the drawing. "What's that?" she asks.

Martin looks at Michael, smiling.

"It's the red bench where he sat when the place blew up. I was there," says Michael. "*Floating.*" Michael buries his head in his hands in disbelief. "That's why he's here, hiding from *them* all these years."

"*That…*," Martin says, "…is where your parents are. And *that*, Michael, is how I'll answer your inquiry."

Martin sluggishly meanders his way to the wooden bed and sits down. He digs into his pile of clothes, pulling out his white lab coat— now yellowed, stained with time. "Help a dying man, would you?" he asks.

"Why should we!" Michael yells.

"I want to expire with whatever remorse I may have left. I want to wear what my faults have forsaken me with. I want to go…*whole* and with sincere regret."

Kyle and Michael begrudgingly hold Martin's frail arms in the air, carefully slipping each coat sleeve to the edge of his wrists.

"Home," says Martin.

Kyle abruptly collapses to the ground, clutching his hearing aid. "They're moving," he says, wincing. "In the distance, they're coming."

"You haven't much time," says Martin, lying on the bed. "Tell me…did my sister make it?"

Kyle shakes his head.

"My brother?"

"He's a gardener," says Skyler.

Martin forms a fake pistol with his hand, cocks back his thumb and releases it in the direction of the kids. "He was the best of us."

"*Guys*, we need to go! They're moving faster, louder." Kyle grimaces, holding onto his ear. "There's hundreds of them. I don't know, maybe thousands."

Martin lays his hands at his sides. "The red...the beauty of the red will guide you. It will flutter with its beacon of life, and protect you. Take the oak to the rock shore and enter through the north gate. Float them all into the water. Float them all but yours. Don't let them reach you. *Now go*!" he screams.

They turn and run through the archway, splashing through puddles in the warehouse. Michael glances back at the archway. *Goodbye Martin*, he mouths. Kyle flinches and grabs his ear, listening to Martin's faint whisper fading into the night.

"*Fly, fly, fly...fly, fly, fly...*"

TWENTY-THREE

THE TOWERS OF GRIEF

Kyle slams shut the warehouse door and limps to his friends, who have been staring at a loud commotion in the street through the chain-link fence.

"You were right, Kyle," says Michael. "They *are* here. And they're coming fast."

Hundreds, perhaps thousands, of dark humanoid shapes steadily march down Front Street toward the Duggan Brothers Steel Mill.

"Shadowpeople!" shouts Nia.

"*No*," replies Kyle. "Just people."

They scamper to the opening in the fence to obtain a better vantage point. The cracked, yellow lamp post bulb that was burned out when they arrived, is now lit, illuminating dangling spiders that have weaved a foreboding message into their web.

They were never against me, whispers Michael, looking at the spiders.

The night-stalking mob creeps ever closer to the mill's entrance, growing more restless with each step. "It's the whole town," says Skyler, befuddled.

Their clothing is ragged, ripped at the seams, and charred with black ash. Their skin, scattered with lesions, some with sloughing skin, and legs that limp like living skeletons, glide methodically toward the fence, like a human tsunami.

"That's Mr. Landis!" shouts Nia.

"Mary Winchester!?" yells Skyler.

Randy, from Randy's Garage limps along, his face nearly unrecognizable.

"This whole time…" says Kyle. "…they were *infected*. No wonder we hardly saw anyone outside. They were hiding."

Skyler squints at an object erratically fluttering above the horde of townspeople, jumping from tree to tree, weaving through flailing arms in the direction of where they are standing.

"*Great,*" says Nia. "Bats."

Skyler pushes to the front, and extends her arm, wet from tear drops that fell into her open palm. "It's a cardinal," she says. "*He came.*"

"Who?" asks Michael.

"Claude—my grandfather!"

The cardinal lands gently on Skyler's

palm, lightly pecking at her skin, nodding, like a chicken scavenging for seed. It's his way of saying hello to his beloved granddaughter.

"The red…" says Kyle. "…the red beauty will guide us."

"This is blowing my mind," says Nia.

"What do we do?" asks Kyle.

"He'll take us to the shoreline," replies Michael. "I saw it in my travels. I just forget where."

The cardinal takes flight from Skyler's hand, hovering above her head, like a helicopter drone. It tilts its head in the direction of the steel mill canal running parallel to the woods leading to the river.

The undead mob walks aggressively faster toward the fenced entrance, knocking those who are weaker and more grotesquely infected to the ground, trampling over them, like a wild herd of maimed buffalo.

Suddenly, a tall man pokes his head out from the middle of the mass. "Hey…Kyle!" he says, smiling.

"*Detective Dansby!*" Kyle shouts.

"Join us," he says. "It's wonderful here." Detective Dansby's smile dissolves into a scowl, and he disappears back into the swarm of infected bodies.

"Go, Claude," shouts Skyler. "Show us the way."

The bird zips ahead, with the friends running behind. They sprint through the night air, doing their best to keep pace with its darting movement. Kyle's pronounced limp prohibits him from catching up. Running alongside the wastewater canal, they anticipate where the cardinal is headed. An old, graffitied rail car that once hauled melded steel, now rusts beside the rope chain entrance to a patch of woods.

"I see him," says Skyler. "Claude, *wait!*"

A dense, rolling fog, seemingly appearing out of thin air, envelops the trees surrounding them. In the distance, near the rail car, moans and groans echo through the trees, ricocheting off decayed drum barrels and corroded steel-mill machinery.

"*Become us!*" screams a sickly voice.

In an instant, crinkled leaves, snapping twigs, and matted crab-grass morphs into the crunching of small, river pebbles. They've made shoreline. The fog partially lifts, but continues floating above the water.

"There it is," Nia says, pointing.

Across the river, about a hundred yards from shore, suspended above the water, like an impenetrable fortress, sits the Marathon Island Nuclear Power Plant. Its perimeter is encased in razor wire, with hulking steam towers reaching into the midnight sky, like colossal, concrete tentacles.

"*Black breeze!*" another voice shouts.

Kyle grabs his hearing aid. "I hear them," he says. "Our parents are in there…*alive.*"

"Claude!" shouts Skyler, peering through the haze. The bird is perched atop a weathered canoe, river waves slapping against its starboard bow.

"That's our ride," says Skyler.

Beside the canoe is an expansive line of dilapidated fishing boats, all missing their motors.

Float them all into the water. Float them all but yours. Kyle winces, hearing Martin's words ring in his ears. "Shove them in, Mike!" he shouts. "Push them all in!"

Like an assembly line, they each grab a boat by the stern and thrust it into the river, watching the current do the rest. They move down the line, heaving all the boats in the river until every last boat is floating downstream. Skyler and Nia jump into the canoe as Michael and Kyle push the stern into the water. They hop in, and begin rowing to Marathon Island. As the canoe drifts toward the rocky island, the ailing mob emerges from the woods, stopping short of the shoreline. They can do nothing but watch the kids float away. "*End shall come!*" yells a voice.

With the last row of the oars, and the mob stranded, for now, across the river, the canoe washes ashore.

"Skyler," says Kyle. "You need to…"

Riiiiiip. Skyler peels the fencing apart, as if prying open an upright sarcophagus. One by one, they duck into the hole and climb up the rock ledge. Claude leads the way. Atop the ledge, the enormity of the nuclear plant reveals itself. Disabled steam towers rise into the starry night like malevolent skyscrapers, dwarfing everything below. They scan the destruction of the industrial landscape until their eyes rest on the genesis of evil.

The red bench.

"That's where it started," says Skyler. It's firehouse-red paint still shimmers against the moonlight, undamaged, and untouched by time.

"Never thought I'd really see it in person," says Michael, remembering his astral projection.

Near the bench is a detached building with a fragmented sign that reads: Maintenance Room.

"That way." Kyle points. "They're crying."

Hearing Kyle, Nia begins sobbing. "Do you really think it's them?" she mumbles through a waterfall of tears. "My daddy's in there?"

"Bust it open, Skyler," Kyle commands.

Whack! With a powerful, overhand hammer-fist, Skyler blasts a hole through the fortified wall. A whirling rush of air backdrafts from within. The light from the moon shines into the room, revealing four pairs of shoes jutting out from the darkness.

Kyle calls out, "Judy!"

"Kyle!" she says.

"Mom," whispers Skyler.

"Michael!" shouts Mrs. Martinez.

"Nia, my flower," mumbles Mr. Park.

The parents, covered in concrete dust, crawl through the hole into the waiting arms of their children.

"How did you…*how did you find us?*" cries Skyler's mom.

Skyler smiles at her friends and rubs her bleeding knuckles. "We had some help, Mama," she replies.

"Are you hurt?" Kyle asks them.

"No," answers his mom. "We were told *they* had bigger plans for us. But now you're here."

"Judy, I…"

"Kyle, what's wrong? *Kyle!*"

Kyle clutches his hearing aid and collapses to the ground, his body convulsing. "They… they're…"

"Kyle!" his mom shouts.

"…*they're here.*"

Along the barbed wire fencing, they stand, menacing, dripping with ashy liquid, gnarled teeth, and sharp, elongated fingernails.

The shadowpeople.

A leader, tall, and much larger than the rest,

slithers forward. The remaining shadowpeople glide through the air, stopping in front of the steam towers, creating a road block for any potential escapees.

The leader opens its decayed jaw. "Your powers are no good here," it says in a dark, other-worldly tone, reaching depths louder and deeper than are possible for human vocal cords. It points to the shoreline across the river. "Poisoned the town. Soon, they'll become *us*."

"What do you want from us?" mumbles Kyle, lying on the ground.

The shadowpeople beside the steam towers slide closer, slowly converging on the children and their parents. The leader steps closer to Kyle.

"We want *him*," it says, revealing its teeth. "Until then, everything dies."

"*Who*!?" shouts Kyle. "Tell us what you want!"

Just then, a figure emerges from within the fog near the shoreline. "*Me*!" it says.

"Martin!" shouts Michael.

The shadowpeople abruptly turn to him, their teeth dripping with rage.

"We thought you died!" says Michael.

"There was one boat left," he says, winking.

"You returned."

"It was the only way."

Martin, dressed in his yellowed lab coat, hobbles gingerly to the leader, who points him to the steam towers. "With us, now," it says.

"*I know*," whispers Martin, accepting his dismal fate.

The leader turns to Kyle, extending its putrefied hand, pointing to the shoreline across the river. "Town shall return."

Kyle, Michael, Nia, and Skyler, along with their parents, watch nervously as Martin, surrounded by shadowpeople, closes his eyes; his head swaying from side to side, he disappears into the fog near the steam towers.

The shadow-people dissipate, leaving behind motionless puddles of black ooze. Kyle grabs his ears and listens as *Lacrimosa* plays one last time. *"All go goodnight into that malicious abyss,"* he mutters. His words cut through the silence of their shared relief, "Let's go home," he says.

TWENTY-FOUR

SMILE

Sunrise. Beams of light trespass through slits in the mini-blinds, brightening Kyle's accomplished face. *I did it.* He walks without limp to the window and twists the curtain rod, fully permitting daybreak to flood the room. *The two towers.* He stares at the distant remnants of Marathon Island, a tragic reminder of carelessness and grief, rising just above the canopy of Cold Creek Forest. Kyle looks down from his third-story window at the street below, and glimpses someone walking by. *Dansby. I wonder what he's doing out so early in the morning?*

Dansby glances up, notices Kyle in the window, and waves.

Kyle gives him a thumbs-up.

Skyler, Michael, and Nia enter the room, having just finished breakfast.

Kyle backs away from the window and sits down on his favorite chair, patting Nia on the head, alerting her of his presence—a queue they had established early on as childhood friends when he'd learned about the Scotopsin buildup that had caused her blindness.

Smirking, Kyle scribbles a note with a large sharpie and holds his message in the air. *I finished it*, the note says.

"That's awesome, Kyle," mouths Michael. "How many pages is it?"

Kyle reads his lips and holds up his fingers, signaling two hundred.

"*How long is his story?*" asks Nia.

"Two hundred pages," replies Michael, loudly. "C'mon, Nia, stop acting like you're blind," he chuckles. Michael takes the pad and scribbles a note to Kyle:

> *Did we win? Did we destroy the*
> *shadowpeople? What happened to*
> *our town? Were we heroes?*

Kyle pauses to write a response, and holds it in the air:

> *Our parents are safe. We used our*
> *superpowers to save them.*

Michael laughs. "I forget. What power did you give me again? I could fly, right? An astral projector? Skyler had like, superhuman strength? Nia could see again, with hawk-like vision. Couldn't she see in ultraviolet light or something cool? And you...you had supersonic hearing?"

Kyle scribbles, *Yep.*

Michael rolls his chair over the hardwood floor to Skyler, who is sitting by the open window watching a cardinal feed from the lunch lady's hand. "Forgot to tell you, Skyler," he says, pushing his finger on her forehead...

HAPPY BIRTHDAY! The big sixteen! You can drive now!"

"Yeah, no doubt, right after my muscular dystrophy is cured," she says, sarcastically. "Maybe you can go with me to the DMV and we can take our driving test together."

"I'm in. I'll just stop being paralyzed."

The entrance door to the common room swings open. "Hey guys," says Judy.

"*Judy!*" they shout.

"Hi, Kyle," she mouths. "How's my favorite teenager doing? You all look so refreshed today. I'll assume breakfast was good?"

"Burritos today," replies Nia. "Mrs. Martinez makes the absolute best yummy ones in this place."

"Yes, she sure does," confirms Judy. "Did you know she's been the head chef here before it was even called the *Recreational Education Center?*"

"This place had another name?"

"What was it called before?" asks Skyler.

"Well, they named it something not exactly friendly to the ears. It was called the *Orphan Asylum for Disabled Children*. Things were different then."

"Was this around the time of the nuclear meltdown on Marathon Island?" asks Skyler. "I heard stories."

"Due in part," replies Judy. "Our town rebounded for the most part. Though, we had a few bumps in the night after the accident."

"What do you mean, *bumps in the night?*"

Judy smiles. "For another day," she says. She walks over to Kyle and gives him a warm hug. "Oh, Kyle, *hey*, your ear is bleeding, honey," she mouths.

Kyle grabs at it and smears blood on his finger.

"I'll get a napkin," she says.

"Is that from his other ear surgeries?" Michael asks.

She wipes Kyle's ear and tucks the napkin into her nursing coat pocket. "Well, I'm hoping all of that stops today. You know what today *is*, Kyle?" she mouths.

Kyle blinks slowly and nods his head.

"You think he'll really hear for the first time? asks Nia. "I wonder what he'll think of our voices? I wonder if he'll listen to X-files re-runs with me?"

Judy turns her back to Kyle so he can't read her lips. "I think this one is going to work. It's a revolutionary new cochlear implant surgery," she says, smiling.

When this surgery was first scheduled, Judy had announced that back when they were kids, nothing like it existed. She had referred to it as "extraordinary and truly experimental." Apparently, Dr. Jenkins is one of the most sought-after surgeons in the country. Ever since he transferred to White Tanks from a prominent clinic in San Francisco, Judy had been raving about him. Still, Kyle is wary. He'd met Dr. Jenkins recently and something about him had felt a bit strange.

Nia slaps her white-tipped cane on the floor and finds her way to Judy. "I hope they invent a revolutionary ocular surgery one day, so I can see the world. I want to see flowers."

"Science will always win," says Judy.

"Yeah, and we're sick of wheelchairs," says Michael, putting his arm around Skyler. "Maybe they can do something for muscular dystrophy and paraplegics."

"Kyle," mouths Judy. "The carrier car will arrive shortly to bring you to the hospital. We're going to get you mildly sedated for prep work. It'll calm you."

Kyle nods.

He scribbles on his notepad and flashes the paper at Judy:

> *My book's done. We beat the*
> *shadowpeople, and saved our parents.*
> *Martin helped us.*

"Fantastic, Kyle. I'll bet he'll be thrilled to hear that he could help" she mouths. "I can't wait to read it! With any luck, maybe *you* can read it to me someday soon." She looks at her watch. "Well, I should go. I'll check in with you all later. I'm going to grab Mr. Grigsby and get Kyle prepped for transport."

Kyle assumes Martin wants to personally oversee the delicate procedure because he's the superintendent.

Michael and Skyler wheel over to the window overlooking the campus grounds. Dansby, dressed in his windbreaker jacket marked SECURITY, is patrolling the sidewalk with his bumbling assistant, Shane Wasser. Dansby is flailing his arms, appearing to reprimand Wasser.

"Wasser always gets the short straw," says Michael.

"He's Dansby's minion," replies Skyler.

Michael looks to his left, and spots the head groundskeeper yanking weeds from the botanical garden.

"Hey, Horner!" yells Michael. "You missed one! *No, not that one.* The one by the tulip!"

Horner stops, sets down his digging spade, and pretends to remove a rifle from around his neck. He aims the gun at Michael, fires, and recoils the barrel.

"Got me!" yells Michael. He looks at Skyler. "I think *he thinks* he's protecting this place. Something is always out to get him."

"Maybe there is," she says, winking.

Kyle walks to the window and places a note on the sill for his friends to read:

> *Gonna miss you guys while I'm over at the stinky place. Always smells like cleaning solution and farts. Doctors freak me out. Wish me luck. I hope I can hear your voices whenever I'm allowed to come back.*

The cardinal perched on the old woman's hand takes flight and lands on Skyler's arm, lightly pecking at her skin, looking for food. Kyle opens the arts and crafts drawer and removes one of the seed sticks they made last week during *Brain Game*, a bi-monthly activity, promoting positive action. He hands it to Skyler.

"Hey, Claude, big day today for Kyle," she says to the bird. Skyler leans out the window and locates the old woman on the bench. "Ruth Ann, *hey*!" she yells…"thanks for sending Claude up to visit!"

The woman, a lunch aid who's fighting skin cancer, smiles, and nods.

"*Fly, fly, fly*…*fly, fly, fly*, Claude."

The common room door swings open, and Judy, accompanied by Martin Grigsby, a tall, gaunt, bony-cheeked man, with long, wispy white hair joins the others by the window.

"Morning, Mr. Grigsby," says Nia.

"Remember, Nia, it's *Martin*," he says with a wink directed at Skyler. "Mister makes me feel so *old*. Kyle, I have your paperwork right here on my clipboard. Your carrier car is in the driveway. It's waiting for a *very* special patient," he mouths.

Kyle nods. He scribbles a short note and

shows it to Judy: *Bye, Mom.*

Judy clutches her heart. "You really know how to make a lady feel special," she mouths. "He's been under my care since he was a baby," she says to Martin. She turns to Kyle. "You're going to hear my voice so much when you return, you'll wish you were deaf again," she mouths.

Kyle gives her a hug.

"Hey, Judy, was Cici down in the office today?" asks Skyler. "I want to talk to her about my fundraising idea for preventing domestic abuse. I got this whole thing planned out in my head."

"No, she isn't," Martin interjects, "but that sounds wonderful. I'm going to personally make a note of it."

Martin grabs Kyle by the hand and escorts him toward the door. "Oh, wait," Martin says. "Nia, hang on." He leaves the room and returns moments later with a gift he retrieves from the hallway. "Mr. Park, the optometrist, wanted you to have this. He asked Horner to pick you a fresh one this morning. It's a purple iris flower from the garden. He said it's, and I quote: *Such a bloom.*"

Nia smiles. "Could you set it on the sill?"

"Of course."

Kyle leans against the wall and snaps a mental memory of his friends. He scribbles a note for them and holds it up:

We're the Flying Tigers. We fly forever. They salute, watching as Judy, Martin, and Kyle exit the common room, leaving the door swaying like a silent metronome.

The carrier car pulls away from the patient drop-off area in front of the hospital. Kyle's mild sedative is making him groggy.

"What do you think of the hospital's new visitor accommodations, Kyle?" asks Martin. "We think the outdoor seating area really brightens the building—wouldn't you agree?"

Kyle, held upright by Judy and Martin,

blinks slowly, his head in a fog. Directly in front of him is a shiny, red bench. "I like to sit here during my visits with other patients. It allows me to observe the chaos that goes on out there," Martin says, smiling, pointing to the city streets. "People running in all directions. It soothes me knowing I am not one of them."

Kyle struggles to decipher the words coming from Martin's moving lips. "We are g-g-going inside now?" he stutters. "My face is…is kind of tingly."

Judy glances at Martin and says something.

Kyle deciphers her comment as concern that the sedative is too strong for his body weight.

"Up we go, dear," says Judy, helping him over a small stoop near the entrance.

The patient registration secretary peeks out from behind her computer screen at Kyle, smiling at Martin. "Right into the elevator on your left," she says. "Dr. Jenkins and his team are all ready for you."

Kyle, almost incoherent, manages a scowl at her. "*I-I-I know her...*"

"He can barely stand," Judy says to Martin. "We need to put him in a wheelchair."

Kyle's eyes flutter open. He groggily scans his surroundings. His body is paralyzed from the anesthesia. At the back of the operating room, he observes several nurses and three doctors talking while removing latex gloves from their hands.

A groan alerts them to his awakening. The surgical team walks to the foot of Kyle's gurney, their hands clasped together in an anticipatory embrace.

Dr. Jenkins grabs a black marker from the surgical tool tray and scribbles onto a white, dry erase board. He holds it up for Kyle:

Can you hear us?

Kyle nods.

The doctors and nurses shake hands.

Dr. Jenkins removes a piece of cloth from his coat pocket and erases the words on the white board. He scribbles another note and holds it up for Kyle:

They'll never believe you, sport.

Dr. Jenkins and his team move closer to Kyle, removing their masks. They smile, revealing long, jagged, pointy teeth.

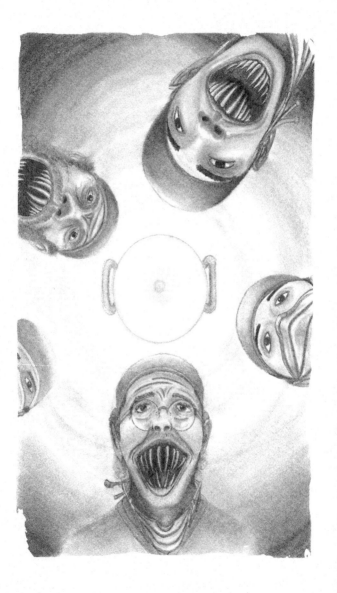

ACKNOWLEDGEMENTS

Tony Maulfair—for sticking with the process, watching it grow, and continuing to amaze readers and myself with your masterful illustrations.

Vanessa Anderson—editor extraordinaire. Your ability to help keep the car on the road while I steer is irreplaceable. NightOwlFreelance.com

Cody Jones—you have provided me with so much help along the way with whatever I've asked regarding photoshop work and miscellaneous art. I appreciate you and your talent.

My childhood friends—Zach, Chris, Mike, James, Tony, Joey, Bruce, Mark, Shane, Phil, Don, Lou, Dave, Jason and many others. You helped inspire this book with our various made-up adventures.

Special thanks to—Cameron, Aubrey, Melisa, Katja DiNunzio, Don Smith, Michelle Smith, Floyd Stokes, Jaci Moos, Roy Combs, Joe Soto, Joe Pizzo, David Snively, Tim Kovaleski, Kelli Perry, Jay Mohr, teachers, librarians, principals, and all the kids who love to read.

This is Main Street in Bressler, my home "Town." My childhood home is just down the block. This picture also inspired the illustration for the front cover.

Cemetery located in Oberlin, PA. My father and grandparents are buried here. The woods in the back inspired the chapter, "Black Breeze."

This is where "Fort Bliss" was built, within Old Man Horner's woods. The real fort was made of old wood planks and nails.

This is where the hose ladder was installed at the top of the hill. We used this steep hill to descend into the creek valley below to where our fort was built.

What remains of The Black Path. It's been closed off, but most of the path is still intact, despite being overgrown with weeds and fallen trees.

This is the old Bethlehem Steel Plant, and
inspiration for Duggan Bros. Steel Mill.

This is "Derndoff's." The original name was Dundoff's. It is across the street from the steel mill, and less than one mile from my childhood home.

Three Mile Island nuclear power plant.

In 1979, a cooling malfunction caused part of the core to melt in reactor #2. The TMI-2 reactor was destroyed. This plant is less than eight miles from my childhood home. I was born three months after the accident occurred.

ALSO BY STEPHEN KOZAN

FOR SCHOOL SPEAKING ENGAGEMENTS

Visit BookVisits.com
or Contact: readyaimwrite@gmail.com
or call: 717.903.9393

More info can also be found at:

www.TownTheBook.com
www.GreatGreenTree.com

Facebook.com/authorstephenkozan

Twitter.com/stephenkozan

To leave a Goodreads review for the
book, please visit Goodreads.com,
and type TOWN by Stephen Kozan in
the search bar.

ABOUT THE AUTHOR

Stephen Kozan grew up around Harrisburg, Pennsylvania, in a small town called Bressler. From an early age, he enjoyed writing and creating stories. His passion for writing started with poetry in grade school, followed by writing music lyrics and short stories in high school. Post graduation, he attended Harrisburg Area Community College, studying literature, and creative writing courses. In addition to publishing *Town*, Stephen also wrote and published *The Great Green Tree And The Magical Ladders*, and *The Journal Of A Lifetime*, which can be found online and in bookstores. He lives in the Harrisburg area with his wife, two children, and dog, Dillon. He can be found at StephenKozan.com.